D0044529

THE STOLEN MAGIC

THE STOLEN MAGIC

LIZ MARSHAM

nelvana

[Imprint]
MAKE YOUR MARK

NEW YORK

[Imprint]
MAKE YOUR MARK

A part of Macmillan Publishing Group, LLC
175 Fifth Avenue, New York, NY 10010

₵nelvana.

Library of Congress Control Number: 2018936698

ISBN 978-1-250-16503-9 (hardcover) / ISBN 978-1-250-16504-6 (ebook)

Our books may be purchased in bulk for promotional, educational, or
business use. Please contact your local bookseller or the Macmillan Corporate
and Premium Sales Department at (800) 221-7945 ext. 5442 or by e-mail at
MacmillanSpecialMarkets@macmillan.com.

Book design by Heather Palisi

Imprint logo designed by Amanda Spielman

First edition, 2018

1 3 5 7 9 10 8 6 4 2

mackids.com

To you who would steal this treasured tale
and rob a bookseller of a sale:
Know that the Mysticons will take back its price
and trap you in a magic prison of ice.

THE STOLEN MAGIC

In Which a Comet Has Its Day,
Magic Goes Away,
and a Belt Gives Way

1

PIPER WAS RIGHT, THOUGHT ZARYA. THIS WAS TURNING INTO A pretty great night.

As the heroic Mysticons, Zarya and her friends—Piper, the acrobatic Mysticon Striker; Em, the steadfast Mysticon Knight; and Arkayna, the inspiring Mysticon Dragon Mage—had been very busy lately. They had discovered that Zarya was not just the clever, sharp-shooting Mysticon Ranger; she was also Arkayna's long-lost twin sister. Though she grew up on the streets, thinking she was an orphan, Zarya, like Arkayna, was actually a princess. Using the power of the Twin Dragons and working with the other Mysticons and their friends, Zarya and Arkayna had overcome the undead Dreadbane, defeated the evil lich queen Necrafa, and saved Drake City . . . and probably all of Gemina.

Zarya shook her head. It made her feel overwhelmed sometimes just thinking about it. But tonight wasn't about fighting thousand-year-old villains, or even thinking about how complicated it was to suddenly be a princess. Tonight was for celebrating . . . and humoring her extremely excited friend.

She tore her eyes away from the performance below to look at the elf girl sitting next to her, and she couldn't help grinning. Piper was completely decked out in Wellsnight memorabilia. A sequined comet shot across the front of her novelty T-shirt, under the words *WELLSNIGHT: THE BEST NIGHT YOU'LL HAVE FOR 70 YEARS!* A mirror ball comet with a shiny tasseled "tail" bobbed back and forth above her head, attached by a spring to her headband. She had even decorated her backpack for the occasion—glitter paint spelled out the words *LIGHT IT UP!*

Piper noticed Zarya's look. "What?" she whispered, putting a hand to her headband. "Is my comet crooked?"

"It's fine; stop fussing with it," Zarya whispered back. "You look great. Very . . . shiny."

Arkayna leaned in from Zarya's other side. "What are you two talking about?" the princess asked. Her long red hair swept around her shoulder as she bent toward them, and a shower of glitter shook free from it. Choko, Zarya's pet foz, was sitting in Zarya's lap and tried to shield himself as the glitter rained down over his huge ears, but there was no escape. He gave a chirrup of resignation and put his now-glittery paws up on the rail in front of them, hoisting himself up to get a better view of the stage.

Zarya sighed. "We're talking 'bout how shiny Piper is, mostly. But you're pretty sparkly yourself, sis."

"You should have let me put some glitter in *your* hair," Piper said, reaching up to run a teasing hand through Zarya's bangs. "You gotta get into the Wellsnight *spirit*! Wells's Comet only comes by—"

"Once every seventy years, I know, Pipes." Zarya chuckled and shook her head at her friend. "You've been talking about it for months."

"Well, you weren't *there* last time!" Piper's eyes went dreamy and distant as she reminisced. "I was only forty, but I still remember how fab-tacular that festival was. It's the best shopping spree and the most scrumptious food and the funnest dancing, all rolled into one, and it goes—"

"All night," finished Zarya along with Piper. "We *know*, Pipes."

"So if you don't get into it, you'll never last until the light show," Piper continued eagerly. "And the light show is the best part! It'll be just before dawn, and you're gonna *think* the party is winding down, but *no*, it's just warming up, because *then*—"

Suddenly Em, who was on Piper's other side, turned to face them. "Then the comet gets so close to Gemina, the Astromancers can bounce their magical lasers off it," she said in a hushed whisper, "and the lasers reflect off the comet and back down into the city in all kinds of patterns and colors, and it will be the most awesome thing we've ever seen. *We know, Piper.*"

Piper blinked.

Em took a deep, calming breath. "Sorry, sorry, sorry," she said. "You've been great at planning tonight. I never would have known what order to do things in without you. I am one lucky dwarf. We all are. Well, we're not all dwarves, but we're all lu—You know what I mean. But"—

she gestured emphatically toward the stage—"we are *missing* the *show*."

"Oh yeah!" replied Piper. The four girls turned to face front. Just as Zarya settled back in her seat, Piper swiped some of the glitter off Choko's head and patted it quickly into Zarya's hair. "You're welcome," Piper whispered in her ear.

Zarya's noise of protest dissolved into an amused snort. Then she refocused on the spectacle in front of her.

If she turned her head to the right from their place in the front row of a section of raised seats, Zarya could see across the plaza to the castle in the background. It was decked out with bunting and banners that shimmered with all the colors of the rainbow. The plaza was just as colorful, filled with food and souvenir vendors and small open spaces where jugglers, dancers, and musicians performed for passersby.

But Zarya's gaze was locked on the space in front of and below her. Tiers of seats, like the ones she and her friends were sitting on, had been set up in an arc facing a wooden stage. The large, wide platform was raised a few feet above ground level, edged by embroidered velvet drapes that swept the flagstones. On both sides of the stage rose wide panels of wood. Carved and painted in sweeping designs, they soared up to support another panel that arced over the stage. This crosspiece was painted with bold, scrolling letters that spelled out *The Amazing Amileth*. Smaller letters down the left panel read *Wonder at Illusions for All Ages*, and a matching design on the right panel said *Experience the Mystery of Magic Without Magic*. Behind this wooden arch, the sides and top of the stage were masked by more sections of velvet, solid red this time, and another thick velvet curtain covered the back. Across the front lip of the stage, a dozen footlights shone up and back, the edges of their beams shimmering strangely. If Zarya listened closely, she could hear them giving off a low, musical hum.

And at the moment she could hear the hum clearly, because the whole audience was waiting, holding its breath. The featured performer of the night, the famous illusionist Amileth, was about to perform one of her best-known tricks. In the center of the stage was a small wooden table with spindly legs. As Zarya watched, Amileth emerged from the velvet drapes on the left, carrying a copper pot. She was wearing her signature outfit, an all-white tailored suit with wide, pointed lapels and long, sweeping coattails. The white fabric shone in the footlights, contrasting dramatically with the red of the velvet and the dark brown of Amileth's skin. Her curly black hair was pulled into a pouf on the top of her head, revealing her long neck and pointed elven ears.

Amileth stopped beside the table, balancing the pot on one hip. She smiled broadly and tipped her head back to address the audience. "Magic, as we know, is not rare in Gemina," she began. "And here in the city, its wonders are all around us. Many of you are carrying it with you tonight, in your handbags, or your phones . . . or maybe, for a few of you, in your very body.

"But with my special footlights, magic is banished from my stage entirely." With her free hand, Amileth gestured to the lights in front of her. "In this anti-magic glow, no spell or charm or hex can survive. And yet, as you will see, magic finds a way to hide . . . in the strangest of places."

Amileth crossed to the lip of the stage and held the pot out, tipping it slightly forward to reveal its contents. "Like dirt!" she announced with a grin. Several members of the audience chuckled.

Zarya leaned forward, straining in her seat, hoping to catch a glimpse of a secret hidden in the crumbly soil. When Amileth spun on her heel, coattails flaring out behind her, Zarya slumped back with a sigh.

Arkayna patted Zarya's shoulder reassuringly. "You knew you weren't going to see anything strange in there," she murmured. "Amileth's too good for that."

"I know, I know," Zarya grumbled. "I just *really* wanna know how she does this one."

Amileth set the pot down on the tabletop and turned back to her audience. "Here in this humble earth," she continued, "we will see that while magic can be buried, it will always flourish." Amileth squared her shoulders and rested a hand behind her back. With her other hand, she reached out over the pot, grasping the air and pulling her fist up slowly. "And it will *thrive*."

Gasps rippled through the audience as green sprouts appeared in the soil and grew rapidly. Leaves unfurled and light pink buds ballooned at the tip of each stem. Amileth spread her fingers wide and intoned, "And it will *breathe*," and the buds burst into the heavy, pink-and-white blossoms of Love's Breath.

Zarya burst into applause along with the rest of the

spectators. Bowing her head slightly to acknowledge the praise, Amileth held her hands out for silence.

"Now, of course," she said wryly, "there's always the possibility that I'm cheating." As the audience laughed, she waved a hand toward the footlights and then the flowers. "So let's put my footlights to the test. If there is no magic on this stage, then these blooms, famed for making most creatures fall instantly in love, will have no effect." She took a step toward the footlights, then turned back to pluck a flower from the pot. Bringing the flower to her nose, she inhaled dramatically . . . then let out her breath in a sighing chuckle. "Of course," she said, shrugging, "elves are immune to Love's Breath, anti-magic lights or no. So I will need a volunteer."

"Ooh!" came a voice from the front row. "Pick me! I command you to pick me!" King Gawayne, Arkayna and Zarya's stepbrother, bounced to his feet, waving his arms impatiently.

"Your Majesty," Amileth replied, arching an eyebrow, "it would be my pleasure." She swept into a deep bow, gesturing with the hand that held the flower to a set of stairs on the side of the stage. "Please join me. But before you do, a warning . . ."

Gawayne was paying no attention, hurrying across the row of seats toward the stairs. Zarya winced in sympathy as, one after another, he managed to step on every single person's toes on the way. The polite citizens tried to muffle their protests, but Gawayne was having none of it. "Make way for the far more important feet of your king!" he complained.

Watching from the stage, Amileth smiled tightly. "Majesty, as I was saying, before you come into the lights—"

But Gawayne still wasn't listening as he tripped over the pointed boots of the lady dwarf on the aisle. "Augh! Is it even legal to have feet that big?" he demanded. "Because I can change that!" Marching up the stairs, he pointed at his butler, who was standing attentively at one side of the audience. "Butler, make a note! Any feet bigger than mine—"

Then Gawayne stepped onto the stage. The hum of the footlights grew louder. With a quiet *tink*, his belt sprang open.

And his pants fell down.

In Which Dances Are Danced
and Theories Are Advanced

2

AS SOON AS GAWAYNE'S ROYAL TROUSERS HIT THE STAGE, the pockets bulged and began spewing forth rings, half-full bottles of star water, a cupcake, four combs, and at least a dozen pairs of sunglasses. Item after item clattered to the wooden boards. Finally, an old, mushy black banana tumbled out of the king's left pocket. A second of quiet passed, and Gawayne stood there, dumbfounded in purple boxers with star lotuses printed on them.

As the audience did their best to smother their laughter, Amileth spread her hands in an apologetic gesture. "As I was telling you, Your Majesty," she said, "if you are carrying anything magical with you—such as, for instance, enchanted pockets of holding—the magic will be removed as soon as the light touches you." She cocked her head to one side as Butler raced onto the stage. "If you don't mind my asking, your belt . . . ?"

"Huh? Oh, yeah, magic belt," said Gawayne, waggling his fingers. "Why should these kingly fingers do anything as boring as buckling a belt? Speaking of which: Butler!"

Butler ran up, already holding a spare non-magical belt. As he fussed over Gawayne, pulling up the king's pants, tucking in his shirt, and replacing his belt, Gawayne peered around him at the detritus. "So what's the deal, lady?" he huffed. "I was saving that cupcake, and now it's got stage all over it. Plus, that was my third-favorite belt, and these are my fourteenth-favorite pair of pants, and you broke them!"

"Oh no, Majesty," Amileth replied. "The footlights suck away magic and store it. As soon as I turn them off, the enchantments will return to your pockets and your belt. They will be good as new, I promise."

Zarya heard Em muttering to herself, "Okay, so the lights hold on to the magic, *that's* how they work."

Leaning across Piper, Zarya said, "That's how she *says*

they work. Which means that's definitely not what they're really doing."

Em raised her eyebrows. "But Gawayne—"

"Ah, she coulda pulled that off easy," Piper put in.

"Yeah, he does love being the center of attention. She had to know he'd volunteer," said Zarya, nodding. "Maybe she got Butler to dress Gawayne in trick pants."

In Zarya's lap, Choko was miming Gawayne's pants falling down and his eyes bugging out in surprise, making Arkayna giggle helplessly. "I don't care what else happens tonight," Arkayna said, "and I don't care how Amileth did it. This is the best thing I've ever seen!"

Zarya nudged Arkayna with an elbow. "You don't care how she did it? You sure?"

Arkayna shrugged. "Well, of *course* I'd like to know," she said. "But sometimes it's nice to *not* know. It's fun to, I don't know . . ."

"Be tricked?" snorted Zarya.

"I wouldn't put it like that, but yeah," agreed Arkayna. "What's the harm in just taking her at her word and being . . . you know, amazed? Isn't that the point of the show?"

"Spoken like a real princess, Princess," Zarya teased.

Zarya hadn't meant to insult her sister, but Arkayna bristled a little. "What's that supposed to mean?"

"Just that, the way I grew up, you needed to know if people were conning you or not," Zarya replied. "You couldn't afford to take someone just at their word."

Arkayna held up a hand in protest. "Hang on, I know the difference between an entertainer and a con artist. I'm not *gullible*."

Zarya winced. "I didn't mean it like that."

"And speaking of you growing up in the Undercity, didn't you used to con people for a living?" Arkayna asked.

Now it was Zarya's turn to be defensive. "I did what I needed to get by, and I never took money from someone who couldn't afford to lose it. Besides, it's like you said. People want to be amazed. So they got the *amazement* of wondering how I tricked them, and I got paid." She grinned. "Everybody won."

"That's not *quite* what I said," Arkayna pointed out.

"Look, the point is, this"—Zarya motioned toward the stage—"is not just a show. It's a *game*. She's outsmarting us. If we don't at least try to figure out how, we lose."

Arkayna opened her mouth to protest, but she was cut off by a commotion from the crowd. Onstage, Butler was standing to one side, laden with an overflowing armload of Gawayne's possessions. The king, meanwhile, had accepted the Love's Breath from Amileth and was raising it to his face.

"Breathe deep, Your Majesty," prompted Amileth.

Gawayne stuck his nose into the flower and inhaled. He lowered his hands, revealing that the tip of his nose was covered in yellow pollen. "Smells like . . . flowers, I guess?" he said, meeting Amileth's eyes.

The audience held their breath.

"Was something supposed to happen?" he asked. He turned the flower upside down and shook it, sending a light dusting of pollen scattering across the stage. "Your flower is broken."

"If you're willing, Majesty," Amileth said, "I'll turn the footlights off and we'll see what happens."

Gawayne sighed. "Fine. But if I walked up all those steps for nothing . . ."

Amileth took a small device out of her pocket and hit a button. The footlights went dark and silent. Then Butler looked down in surprise as Gawayne's magic belt, deep in the pile of belongings he held, buzzed musically for a moment. Gawayne's pants, too, gave off a low drone as the

16

magic returned to their pockets. And the Love's Breath blossom and the pollen on Gawayne's nose began to hum and glow as the magic within them stirred to life.

"Uh-oh," Zarya and Arkayna muttered in unison.

"Hey, that tickles," Gawayne said, swiping at his nose. "What—" He looked into the audience and locked eyes, through a drift of dancing, glowing pollen, with the booted dwarf lady on the aisle. "You," he breathed, "have the most *perfect feet.*"

The dwarf lady inhaled in surprise. As she did, she sucked in one of the glowing motes of pollen that was drifting off the stage. She blinked, then rose and put her hands to her heart, gazing moonily at Gawayne as she hurried up the steps. "But I would gladly shrink them away to nothing, if only you asked it," she replied.

"You see?" announced Amileth. "Love, like magic, will always thrive! Let's give them a big hand!"

While the audience burst into thunderous applause, Gawayne and the dwarf reached for each other and proceeded to tango dramatically into the wings.

Amileth raised her voice to be heard over the cheering. "And now, while we give the Love's Breath a minute to wear off, a short intermission!" She bowed deeply as a thick red curtain dropped from the wooden arch to cover the stage.

"Okay," said Em. "I admit it. I have no idea how she did that!"

"I thought for sure the flower was fake," Piper said. "But then when it suddenly glowed . . . hoo!" She shook her head. "That girl is *good*."

"Wouldn't it be weird if the footlights actually worked?" mused Arkayna.

Choko made a skeptical noise, wrinkling his nose.

"No way they work," Zarya agreed. "No *way* she invented something that sucks away magic just to put on a show."

Em nodded in agreement. "It'd be way too powerful for her just to use it like this," she said. "There's gotta be something we're missing."

The girls continued to debate their theories, but Zarya was distracted by her earlier conversation with Arkayna. Did her sister really judge her for the way she used to make money? *Arkayna would have done the same thing in my place*, Zarya told herself. *We're different, yeah, but we're not that different.*

She was brought back to the present by Piper excitedly

drumming on her arm as Choko hopped up and down in her lap. "It's starting, it's starting, it's starting!" Piper hissed.

The curtain swept up, revealing Amileth standing center stage. To the left of her was a large, deep cabinet, its doors hanging open to reveal a simple wooden chair inside. Behind her, stretching off to the right side of the stage, was a long table, fully set for a banquet. Candles flickered, and food was piled invitingly on serving platters, but there were no chairs.

"For my next series of illusions," Amileth said, "I'm going to need three more volunteers. And don't worry! No more magical plants, I promise."

The crowd laughed, and hands shot into the air. No one was more eager, though, than Zarya, who was squirming around in her seat, trying to get a better look at the cabinet and table over Choko's large ears.

Amileth's eyes swept the seats. She pointed at a burly dwarven man, then at an elderly elven woman. Then she raised her eyes to the upper tiers, looking for the final volunteer, and grinned.

"It appears another member of the royal family wants to be part of the show," she said, waving a hand to where the girls sat. "Come and join me, if you would, Princess."

Zarya slumped. *Of course,* she thought, *Arkayna would be the one who got chosen. She doesn't even really care about—*

"Hey," Arkayna said, nudging Zarya. "What's wrong? Get down there." When Zarya looked at her, startled, Arkayna laughed. "You thought she meant me, didn't you? Think again, *Princess,*" she teased.

Zarya looked down at the stage. Sure enough, Amileth wasn't beckoning to Arkayna. The illusionist was looking directly at *her.*

In Which Zarya Searches for
Secrets and Finds a Flaw

3

STEPPING INTO THE FOOTLIGHTS, ZARYA DIDN'T KNOW WHERE to look first. The empty cabinet beckoned invitingly; she was *sure* she could find a hidden mirror or trapdoor in there. But the table—what was going to happen with the table? Or maybe she should focus on the lights?

"Ah, Princess Zarya," Amileth said, coming toward Zarya with her hand outstretched. "Such a pleasure to have you on my stage. I hope you left all your magical items with your friends?"

Zarya nodded, pointing to where Choko stood on the railing in front of their seats, waving Zarya's phone.

Smiling warmly, Amileth shook Zarya's hand in a firm, friendly grip, then led her to a spot in front of the cabinet where the other volunteers were already waiting. Turning to address the crowd, she continued, "The first thing I will ask my kind volunteers to do tonight is"—she dropped Zarya's hand, reached into the inside pocket of her jacket, and pulled out a length of black silk cord—"tie me up!"

The dwarven man and elven woman were hesitant, but Zarya immediately reached for the cord. "Let's do this!" she said.

Amileth quirked an eyebrow, reading the challenge in Zarya's eyes, then nodded and led Zarya to the chair inside the cabinet. Amileth sat down, threading the rope behind her bent knees. She crossed the rope over itself, then handed the ends to Zarya. Then she placed her wrists, one over the other, across the rope. "Pull as tightly as you like," instructed Amileth, her voice loud enough to carry to the entire audience. "Then tie the ends around my wrists and knot them, please, Princess. Use any knot you please. The knot is immaterial, because in a few moments . . . I will also be immaterial! That's right, watchful viewers, once these cabinet doors are closed, I will demonstrate that the rules of solid matter need not apply to me. I will, without magic, phase through these cords, this chair, and the very cabinet itself!"

As Amileth spoke, Zarya eyed the way the rope was wrapped around the illusionist's legs, and the way her hands were stacked. She met Amileth's eyes and smiled again, reaching forward to try to adjust the position of the illusionist's wrists. In an instant, Amileth's smile became more fixed, and she held herself firmly in place. Zarya knew she had figured out how the trick worked—the way Amileth had arranged herself and the rope, she would easily be able to twist out of whichever knot Zarya tied without untying it.

But Zarya wasn't there to mess up the show. Quickly, she tied Amileth's wrists together in an elaborate, strong knot. "You're not getting out of this in a hurry," she told Amileth loudly. Then, with her back to everyone else as she tugged one last time on the cord, Zarya gave the illusionist a private wink. Amileth's face relaxed, and Zarya heard her breathe a soft, relieved laugh.

As Zarya stepped out of the cabinet, Amileth instructed the other volunteers to come forward and inspect the knot. When both of them had proclaimed it to be tight and sturdy, Amileth asked them to close the cabinet doors, step away, and count to five.

The dwarf swung the doors closed with a solid *chunk*, cutting off everyone's view of Amileth. Zarya and the other two volunteers backed toward the lip of the stage, and together the crowd began to count. "One . . . two . . . three . . . f—"

Ka-chunk! The doors swung open, revealing . . . nothing but the chair and the cord! As the audience gasped, Amileth strolled out from behind the cabinet with her arms held wide. She swept up the cord and held it over her head, displaying that it was still tightly knotted, as everyone cheered and clapped.

For her next trick, with the volunteers still onstage, Amileth made all the dishes on the table levitate. She told a whimsical story about a party of ghosts coming to dine, and the audience was enraptured by both the tale and the trick. All except Zarya, who noticed that whenever Amileth waved one hand in a flashy gesture, the other would steal into her pocket or behind her back.

I bet she's got that device from earlier up her sleeve, Zarya realized. She started looking around for hidden mechanisms when all other eyes were on Amileth, and soon enough she caught the telltale glint of a hidden, hair-thin wire above one of the candlesticks. She allowed herself a small smirk, proud at having discovered the secret. Then she noticed that Amileth was looking right at her. Zarya gave the illusionist a subtle nod. *I'm not going to say anything,* Zarya wanted to convey, *I just want to know how you're doing all this.*

But Amileth didn't seem as relieved this time. Zarya noticed, as the elf moved back across the stage to the cabinet, that her patter was a little less fluid, a little more forced.

"For my final illusion," Amileth said, her eyes darting to Zarya every few seconds, "I will transport one of you brave volunteers into the spirit realm and then back again. I will need to blindfold you, for the spirit realm holds many wonders not meant for our mortal eyes. Which of you is brave enough to take the journey? You, sir!" She moved toward the dwarf immediately, not giving Zarya any time to respond. "You seem an intrepid sort, would you agree?"

Zarya chuckled quietly. Put like that, who would say no? Sure enough, the man took a deep breath, stepped into the cabinet, and allowed himself to be blindfolded.

As Amileth continued spinning the tale of the mystical, but not magical, journey he was about to take, Zarya's eyes raked the inside of the cabinet. If the volunteer wasn't in on the trick, then he wasn't actually going to move, which meant the cabinet needed to be . . . There, she saw the secret!

The top of the cabinet was just a bit thicker than the sides, and a faint but unmistakable line ran across the ceiling. It had to be a hinge.

Once the cabinet door was shut, Zarya was betting that an angled mirror would drop down. It would cut the space inside the cabinet in two, sealing the dwarf away, and reflecting the remaining empty part to make the entire cabinet appear empty. The blindfolded man would feel a rush of air from the mirror but would otherwise have no idea what was going on.

Zarya's gaze dropped to the floor of the cabinet to see if she could tell where the mirror would land. Sure enough, a faint guideline ran diagonally across the wood . . . and the dwarf's foot rested right on top of it.

She looked up at Amileth in alarm. But Amileth was so distracted by Zarya, she hadn't noticed that her volunteer wasn't fully in place. If the mirror dropped now, his foot would be crushed!

*In Which There Are Invitations
and Consternation*

4

ZARYA SPOKE UP QUICKLY. "OPENING PORTALS TO THE SPIRIT realm is no joke," she said. "You're sure we're all safe here?"

Amileth furrowed her brow for a moment, puzzled, then smiled reassuringly. "You're perfectly safe, Princess," she replied.

"Okay," said Zarya, leaning forward a bit and giving the dwarf a significant glance, "so we're *all* right where we *should* be?"

Following Zarya's glance, Amileth noticed the placement of the man's foot inside the cabinet. She gave a little gasp, which she quickly turned into a clearing of her throat. "I assure you, Princess," she said smoothly, "that all will be well."

Amileth stepped inside the cabinet and turned to the dwarf. "Sir, let me give your blindfold one last adjustment . . ." After fussing with the blindfold for a moment, she took hold of his shoulders, as if she was adjusting his jacket. While doing so, she pushed him lightly backward, making him shift his feet to keep his balance. "Sorry, sir," she continued. "Just sprucing you up. We want you to look your best when the spirits see you, don't we?"

As Amileth backed out of the cabinet, Zarya saw her give the volunteer one last look. His feet were now perfectly in place. She nodded firmly, closed the cabinet doors, and proceeded with the illusion.

When Amileth opened the doors a few seconds later, the cabinet appeared completely empty. Amileth took her bow to the resulting applause, then began spinning a tale of what strange sights awaited the dwarf in the spirit realm should he be foolish enough to remove the blindfold. "And so, for safety and sanity, his brief journey must come to an end," she concluded. *"Now."*

She swung the doors wide again. Colored smoke billowed out of the cabinet and curled across the stage floor, revealing the blindfolded volunteer standing inside. In the standing ovation that followed, Amileth ceremoniously whipped the blindfold from his eyes, led him forward, and had him take a bow. She shook hands with him, then with the elderly woman, and lastly with Zarya. Then, to continued applause, Amileth led the volunteers to the steps and gestured that they should descend into the audience again.

As Zarya passed by Amileth and headed down the stairs, she felt the illusionist's arm brush her side. "Thank you," Amileth said under her breath, giving Zarya a last, dazzling smile.

Zarya's heart was beating fast as she made her way through the exiting crowd. As soon as she knew no one was paying attention, she checked her pockets. In her hoodie, on the side where Amileth had brushed her, was a small piece of parchment. *Meet me in an hour,* it said, with directions to a small field nearby.

Unable to help herself, she spun back to look at the stage . . . only it wasn't a stage anymore. The curtain had dropped, and the whole wooden apparatus seemed to be twisting and folding in on itself. Zarya stepped out of the stream of people and stood on the nearest seat to get a better look.

"Oh yeah," said a man standing nearby in the same row of seats. "This is just as good as the rest of the show. Don't know why everyone doesn't stay to watch; they all think it's magic, but I'm pretty sure it's not. Anyway, the whole thing folds up and turns into a truck. Which is also her house. Isn't that something?"

"Wow," Zarya breathed, impressed. "Em must be *loving* this." She craned her neck around, looking for her friends. Sure enough, Em was standing frozen at her seat, mouth open. Next to her, Piper stood with Choko on her shoulder, both of them mimicking Em's stunned pose.

Zarya waved and caught Piper's eye. *I'll come to you,* she mouthed. Piper raised a hand in a thumbs-up.

A minute later, Zarya rejoined her friends in their seats. The painted arch that defined the top of the stage had lowered, and the sides had fully collapsed into the deck. Now the whole deck hinged along its length, folding upward behind the arch. One side extruded itself, unfolding into what quickly became recognizable as the cab of a vehicle, and the embroidered curtain along the front of the stage hitched up to reveal large wheels.

Now the four girls gazed at a large wooden trailer with *The Amazing Amileth* painted along its side. With one final wave, Amileth jumped into the cab and began slowly inching her trailer through the crowd and away from the festival.

"Wasn't she just fab-tacular?" asked Piper, clapping her hands. "Now, if we hurry, we can get in another round of snacks before the face-painting booths open!"

Choko nodded eagerly and patted his belly, always in favor of a plan that involved snacks.

"Piper, that sounds amazing, but look." Zarya showed Piper the note. "Choko, can I have my phone back? In this crowd it's gonna take me almost an hour to get over there, and I don't want to be late."

"*What?* But . . . but . . ." Piper trailed off, reading and rereading the note. "You can't go!"

"Why not?" asked Zarya in surprise.

"Because! Because . . . she's tricky!"

"She's what?" Zarya asked. "You called her *fab-tacular*, like, ten seconds ago!"

"Well, she is fab-tacular," Piper retorted, "but she's also . . . sneaky! Or . . . something!"

"Piper," said Em gently. "Is this maybe not about Amileth? Maybe this is about how you had a plan for all of us to do the festival just like you did last time, and now Zarya's going off by herself for a bit?"

"No!" Piper said firmly. Then she drooped. "Maybe." She took Zarya's phone from Choko and handed it over, peering up at her. "So hurry, okay? You can't be the only one without face paint. That'd be the worst."

Zarya grinned. "The worst, huh? Can't have that. I'll be back soon, promise."

Then Arkayna spoke up. "I don't see why we can't *all* visit Amileth."

Zarya's stomach tightened. She really wanted to go on her own. She loved her friends and her sister, but right now she just wanted part of the night to feel like . . . hers. But she couldn't say that to Arkayna. So instead she said, "Well, I was the only one invited. And she's supposed to be really secretive, right? So—"

Arkayna frowned. "But if she's gonna share secrets with you, why can't we all know them?"

"Arkayna," said Em in that same gentle tone. "Now

that Zarya's a princess, she's going to get singled out for special attention sometimes, too. And that's a good thing. Right?"

Arkayna's eyes widened. "Of course it is! I didn't mean . . . You're right, Em. Zarya, you should go."

Zarya chucked Em on the shoulder. "You're pretty smart, there."

"Oh, don't get me wrong," Em replied. "I would sell my last wrench for a chance to see inside that wagon of hers. I am *seething* with envy." She shrugged and smiled, totally relaxed. "But you should still go."

"Okay. As long as we're good?" Zarya looked at Em, who nodded. Piper and Choko gave her a quadruple-thumbs-up.

Then Arkayna pulled her into a hug. "We're *always* good," she said. "Have fun."

A little while later, Zarya approached Amileth's trailer. It was as long as the stage had been wide and about half as tall, and light shone from a series of small windows along its top. There was no one in the cab, so Zarya made her way around to the back, listening to the strange humming and chugging noises coming from inside. Where most trucks would have huge roll-up doors, a short collapsible staircase instead led to a small, plain door with a metal handle.

"Hello?" Zarya called, tapping on the door. *"Hello?"* She knocked more forcefully.

No answer.

She reached down and tried the handle. The door was unlocked. Zarya opened it a crack and stuck her head through . . . and gasped.

The inside of the trailer didn't look like the stage. It didn't look like a house, either. And it didn't look like any vehicle or storage space Zarya had ever seen. Stacks of crates were piled against the walls, out of which spilled rope, cables, scarves, curtains, pieces of wood and metal, and some things Zarya couldn't make out. Among the crates, Amileth's completed tricks were disassembled and stacked; Zarya recognized the pot and table for the Love's Breath illusion and the dishes for the banquet levitation, half-packed away. One whole corner was devoted to a giant pegboard, on which hung dozens of differently sized wrenches, screwdrivers, hammers, saws, and chisels. Another corner was curtained and lit like a smaller version of Amileth's stage, and a table with strange metal tubes around it gleamed under the theatrical lights. Workbenches were scattered around the room, and on each one a different project was partially assembled. All of them looked fascinating, and Zarya had no idea what any of them were for.

It looked like a fully functioning, cluttered, busy workshop. In other words, it looked like Em's dream home.

"Oh, Em is gonna *kill me*," Zarya breathed.

"You're here!" Amileth called, coming out from behind some kind of contraption Zarya couldn't identify—it looked like the top half of a metal titan? Maybe?—and wiping her hands on a rag. Her jacket was off, her sleeves were rolled up, and Zarya noticed absently that while her fingers were covered in grease, the rest of her white outfit was immaculate.

"Yeah, but what is *here*? I thought this was where you lived, but . . ." Zarya gestured helplessly around her.

"It is!" said Amileth brightly. Looking much more casual and at ease than she had been onstage, she pointed to the pegboard corner. "At least while I'm touring. My bedroll is over there. Living doesn't take up much space. Not like working. I have to work all the time to make sure my act is perfect. There's no room for error." She heaved a sigh, shaking her head. "But still, I would have botched a very important performance, not to mention hurt someone, if it weren't for you. And that's why I asked you here."

"To thank me?"

"Well, yes. But also, tonight made me realize that my act is missing something crucial. My illusions are getting more complicated, and it's a lot for one person to keep track of. I need someone to watch my back. Someone smart, someone who can think on her feet better than I can. I need a partner."

Amileth stepped forward and took Zarya's hands. "I need you, Zarya."

In Which There Is a
Shocking Development

5

ZARYA'S MIND WHIRLED. OF COURSE SHE WASN'T GOING TO leave everything behind—her friends, her newly found family, her duty as a Mysticon, her whole life—to become an illusionist. But something about the offer made her wistful. Maybe it was that, not so long ago, she would have jumped at a chance like this.

"Hey," Amileth said, lightly shaking Zarya's hands and peering teasingly into her eyes. "Anyone in there?"

Zarya blinked and realized she'd been staring off into space. "Sorry, Amileth—" she began.

"Oh, please, call me Ami!"

"Ami, okay. It's just . . . it's mind-blowing that you would even ask me," Zarya stammered. "A few years ago, my friend Piper and I were running games on Undercity street corners for spare change. Just little sleight-of-hand tricks. I never could have pulled off anything like you do, growing flowers and making Gawayne's pants explode and stuff." She chuckled at the memory. "How did you do that, by the way, can I ask? It's killing me."

Ami dropped Zarya's hands and crossed her arms. "Ahhh, you want to know *all* my secrets right away, just like that? So you're taking the job?"

"Oh!" Zarya faltered, embarrassed. "No, you're right, sorry, I shouldn't have asked. Part of me wishes I could go with you, but—"

Ami burst out laughing. "I was teasing you, Princess. I'm happy to tell you the truth, which is the same thing I tell everyone: The footlights work."

"Wait. The footlights . . . you invented anti-magic lights, for real?" Zarya couldn't believe it. "But . . . but . . ."

"Why don't I make them into a weapon?" Ami asked. "Why aren't I worried that someone else will?"

"Yeah!" Zarya sputtered.

"The second question is easy: You see yourself that

no one believes me. They all assume I'm lying, because the truth is too simple. I do this"—she gestured around her—"in the hardest way possible: with practical effects, a ton of practice, and zero magic." She walked over to a table and picked up a long, thin tube with a small nozzle at one end and a thumb-size black box at the other. "As for the first question, why *would* I make weapons? Weapons don't interest me. Do you know why I do what I do?"

"Sure." Zarya shrugged. "I was talking with Arkayna about this. It's a game."

"A game!" Amileth seemed genuinely surprised. She slipped the black box into her back pocket and looped the tube around her neck, letting the nozzle drape down one arm. "No, it's not a game. Though it may have started out that way. I was born into a very magical family, you see, but I have no magic in me at all."

She crossed to the pegboard, pulled her jacket off a hook, and put it on, threading the tube through one arm so the nozzle rested invisibly against her wrist. "The pressure was tremendous. 'Make your bed without using your hands.' 'Light a fire without using a match.' Week after week, year after year, I could feel their disappointment in me. Until I decided to find my own way. One day, they told me to light a fire, and"—she held up her hand with a flourish, and a small gout of flame *poof*ed from the nozzle and hovered above her palm—"I did."

"See?" said Zarya. "You outsmarted them. It was a game, and you won. Nice job!"

"Thank you, but I'm not finished. You see, my new 'magic' stopped my family from being disappointed, but it didn't make them proud. I was only doing what was expected of me. And I realized: I want to do *unexpected* things. I want people to walk away from my shows full of wonder. I don't want to play a game; I want to create a *story*, a fantasy so interesting that even though they know it's false, they'll choose, if only for a minute, to believe it anyway. And they'll walk away remembering that there's more to life than they think." With that, Ami shrugged off her jacket to reveal that instead of the tube, a snake now hung around her neck.

Zarya jumped and bit back a yelp.

"See?" Ami reached up and pulled the snake into her hands. "You know it can't be real, and yet . . ."

Zarya leaned forward as Ami flipped the "snake" over and revealed a metal seam in its belly. Ami pried the seam open with her fingernails, revealing the tube hidden inside. The "snake" was a spring-loaded casing, painted to look like a snake and probably hidden inside Ami's jacket, ready to snap into place at her command.

"I will admit, though," Ami continued, "I do enjoy when someone like King Gawayne volunteers. People with easy lives always assume they know how everything works. I think it's healthy for them to remember otherwise." She seemed to suddenly realize whom she was talking to, and met Zarya's eyes sheepishly. "I hope you don't mind me saying so. Princess."

Now it was Zarya's turn to laugh. "Are you kidding? I want you to move here and do that to him twice a week!"

Ami chuckled along with her. "I didn't know you grew up in the Undercity," she said, "but it doesn't surprise me. You don't act like any princess I've ever met. And that's a compliment." She put a hand on Zarya's shoulder, smiling ruefully. "Please don't change. People who have money, or magic, or both—they don't know what it's like for those of us who don't. You keep reminding them, okay?"

Zarya stiffened, suddenly uncomfortable. After all, not only did she have money now, she had magic—Mysticon magic. *We have even less in common than she thinks,* Zarya thought. Out loud she said, "Aw, Arkayna's not so bad. And she's been through some rough stuff, too."

"Yes, of course." Ami dropped her hand and looked chastened. "Her—*your*—poor parents. Is it true they were turned to bone? I've been away for months, and the news is sometimes exaggerated."

"It's true," Zarya said sadly.

Ami took a deep breath. "Well," she said. "I have brought down the mood. Allow me to make it up to you." She motioned to the workbenches around her. "How about a tour?"

"Even if I can't run away with you?" Zarya asked.

"Even if. What would you like to see first?"

Zarya pointed at the metal titan. "That. For sure."

Over the next hour, Ami walked Zarya around the workshop, showing her the various mechanisms she used to produce magical effects. The titan was a complicated automaton that, if Ami could get it working, would appear to speak and identify items audience members held up. In reality, Ami would be remote controlling it through valves that ran under the stage.

The Love's Breath trick turned out to be incredibly

complicated: An angled mirror under the spindly table hid a pipe reaching up from the floor to the bottom of the flowerpot; a series of nested tubes and cleverly folded bundles of tissue paper pushed up through the pipe, through the soil in the pot, and unfurled into lifelike plants; and a hidden compartment in Ami's sleeve allowed her to deftly swap out a tissue paper flower for a real one before the volunteer could touch it.

Zarya had expected to be a little disappointed once she knew the secrets—usually tricks seemed so obvious after someone explained them to you—but instead she found herself even more impressed with Ami. The elf girl was so clever and so good with her hands, and she seemed to know exactly where her audience would be looking at any moment.

"Another of my secrets, of course, is also hiding in plain sight." Ami drew the device she had used onstage out of her pocket. The top had two large switches on it, labeled CURTAIN and LIGHTS. "The audience sees me use this to lower the curtain and control the lights, and they assume that's all it does. No one thinks that maybe it could do more. Maybe it could, in fact, control the whole show." She turned the device over to reveal dozens of tiny buttons on its underside, each smaller than a fingernail. The buttons were unlabeled and painted to look exactly like the rest of the device's housing. Even from a foot away, Zarya had trouble making them out.

"I *knew* I saw you reach into your pocket!" Zarya crowed.

"Yes, you have very clever eyes," responded Ami. "Actually, before you go, I could use those eyes." She pointed at the curtained area, where the metal table waited. "Would you mind giving me some advice on this?"

Zarya felt a little guilty about how long she had already been away, but she was so curious. "I can spare *one* more minute," she said.

"Good." Ami pointed to a nearby workbench. "Leave your phone there, please, and any other magic items you have on you. I'd like you to see this with full lighting, so you can tell me if it works."

Obligingly, Zarya dropped her phone onto the bench. Then together, they stepped into the lights.

"I was going to perform this tonight," Ami confessed, "but I don't think it's ready." She pointed to the table. "A volunteer lies there, and I tell them that with the power of their mind they can make the whole tabletop float with them on it. I have them concentrate very hard, you see, with their eyes shut tight." She pushed a button on the bottom of her device, and a metal pipe with a large C-shaped curve at the end rose from the floor behind the table. "I stand here," she said, stepping between the pipe and the table, "which blocks the audience from seeing what's happening. So the visuals are fine. But I worry that the volunteer will feel . . ." She pointed, and they watched as the tube rotated so that the C-curve wrapped around Ami's waist and attached itself to the table, making the metal surface judder slightly. ". . . that. The pipe needs to attach to the table so it can lift it, but that shaking is going to give me away."

Zarya whistled. The trick was beautifully designed. The pipe was completely hidden by the table as it came out from behind Ami and grabbed on, and from there it was a simple matter of raising and lowering it—and the tabletop and volunteer along with it. They would really look like they were levitating.

Zarya hopped up on the tabletop. "Well," she said. "Let's try it!"

"Excellent." Ami grinned and pushed another button, but nothing happened. She frowned and pushed the same button again. Still nothing. "That should have disengaged the pipe," she muttered. "I'm still wiring this thing up." She passed the device to Zarya. "Hold this for a minute? I'm going to grab a screwdriver."

As Ami headed toward the pegboard, Zarya turned the device idly in her hands. Then she froze and looked closer. The malfunctioning button was slightly out of alignment with the others, she realized.

"Hey, I think I found the problem," Zarya called. "What if I just—"

She pushed the button back into alignment. With a sharp *screech*, the pipe separated from the table, throwing up sparks. One of the sparks hit the device in Zarya's hand, causing a short circuit that traveled through Zarya and down to the metal table she was sitting on.

But Zarya had no time to think about what was happening in detail. She was too busy being electrocuted.

In Which Most of Zarya
Goes Home

6

"ZARYA!" AMI SHOUTED. SHE BOUNDED ACROSS THE WORK-
shop in four long strides, grabbing a wooden pole as she
ran, and batted the device out of Zarya's hand. With the
circuit broken, the electricity was dissipated, and Zarya
slumped to the table. Ami shot out an arm, grabbing
Zarya's head before it could hit the metal and laying her
down gently.

"Are you all right? Please say you're all right!" Ami
cried.

"Whoa, yeah, I'm okay," mumbled Zarya, pushing herself up to a sitting position. She took a few deep breaths

and shook herself a bit. "Yeah. I'm fine. Takes more than that to rattle my cage."

"I can't believe that happened; I am so, so sorry." The elf girl wrung her hands, flustered and near tears.

Zarya was immediately self-conscious. The last thing she wanted was to be cried over. "Oh, hey, don't worry about it," she assured her. "It was an accident!"

Ami shook her head. "It never should have happened. I'm going to check all the wiring as soon as I get home." Then she brightened. "Speaking of which, you should come and visit me! This was my last show for a few months, so I'm heading to my house right from here. My *real* house. I live in the exact center of the Weaving Woods, and you're welcome anytime."

She raised a playful eyebrow and deepened her voice dramatically. Now she sounded the way she did onstage. "And I must warn you, Princess. The way is heavily booby-trapped to turn aside those who would uncover my wondrous secrets!"

She laughed, and her tone became light again. "But I know that with your skills, you'll have no trouble finding me."

Zarya grinned hugely. She knew a challenge when she

heard one. "You're on, Ami. See you soon." She jumped off the table, grabbed her phone, and headed for the door.

Back at the Stronghold, Arkayna, Em, and Piper listened closely, with freshly painted faces, to Zarya's story. Choko listened, too, as well as he could in between bites from his huge pile of snacks. Em kept stopping Zarya to ask for more details, and Zarya was happy to gush about how Ami pulled off each illusion. But when Zarya got to the part where Amileth was demonstrating the table levitation, she noticed that Piper was drooping a bit.

"What's up, Pipes?" Zarya asked. "I'm sorry I missed the face paint. But look at it this way: We're going on patrol in a minute, and the paint would have come off then anyway. Right?"

"It's not that," Piper grumbled. "I mean, it *is* that. I really wanted to see you with a big comet painted on your forehead. But also . . . *ugh*." The little elf threw up her hands. "I'm happy that you like her! For realsies! But you and I do tricks together; that's *our* thing. Can't you have a different thing with her?"

"Aw, Pipes," Zarya said. "Don't worry. That will always be our thing! I didn't even end up helping her at all—I just got myself shocked!"

"You *what*?" demanded Arkayna.

Piper put her hands to her face and mimed being surprised. "You mean 'shocked' like *'Eeeee!'* or 'shocked' like . . ." She jerked her body around spasmodically.

"The second one," said Zarya. "Although kinda both?"

Arkayna strode to Zarya's side and looked her over closely. "Were you hurt? What did she do to you?"

"Easy there, sis, I'm okay." Zarya held out her hands in a placating gesture, and Choko took the opportunity to leap into her arms and crawl up to her shoulder, his tail wrapping around her neck possessively. "And she didn't *do* anything. It was an accident." She patted Choko fondly. "I'm *fine*, buddy."

Choko sniffed her hand, shrugged, and jumped back down to his pile of snacks.

"See?" Zarya said. "Choko thinks I'm fine."

"Look, I know you want this girl to be wonderful, and I know you two have a ton in common," said Arkayna. "But everything in that truck is her responsibility, so it's her fault you got hurt! Also," she continued, raising a finger, "if you had let us come with you, this probably wouldn't have happened."

Zarya took a deep breath. She knew Arkayna didn't mean to be bossy. Her sister was just concerned, and maybe a little jealous. So Zarya held out her hand, and Arkayna took it. "I am totally okay," Zarya said. "Really."

Arkayna finally relaxed. "All right," she said. "I believe you." She straightened her shoulders. "Girls, it's time for patrol, and you know what that means. It's magic hour!"

Raising her arms, Arkayna summoned her Mysticon magic. A wave of green energy transformed her clothes into the white, green, and gold outfit of the Mysticon Dragon Mage. A long gold staff topped with a glowing orb appeared in her hand, and a green mask covered her eyes.

"Let's go!" Em held her hands out in front of her, calling upon her powers as the Mysticon Knight. A shining pink sword appeared in her grasp, and a ripple of pink energy washed over her, leaving her dressed and masked in pinks and purples.

"Woo-hoo!" Piper clapped and capered as orange magic swept from her head to her toes. Newly dressed in her orange, teal, and white Mysticon Striker outfit, she summoned her sparkling golden hoops and began juggling them. Closing her eyes behind her teal mask, she shouted, "And for our next trick, a blind back somersault toss-a-riffic target special!" She turned a neat backflip, eyes still closed, and threw her three hoops up in the air. "There's your target, Ranger!"

"You got it, Striker!" Zarya opened her hand to summon her magical bow, already eyeing the trajectory she'd need to get an arrow through all three hoops.

Her hand stayed empty. A second later, Piper's hoops clattered to the ground.

"Huh?" Piper opened her eyes. "What happened?"

"I'm not sure." Zarya closed her hand, shook it, and then opened it again. Still, her hand was empty.

"Zarya," said Arkayna, a tense edge to her voice. "What's going on?"

"Nothing. I told you, I'm fine," snapped Zarya. She held both hands out in front of her and stared at them, concentrating. "Mysticon Ranger!" she demanded. But nothing happened. No familiar tingle of energy. No rush of power.

"Oh no." Em put a hand to her head. "Zarya, you are not fine."

Zarya looked up, fear in her eyes. "You're right. My magic is gone."

In Which a Truck Leaves a Trace,
but a Mysticon Vanishes

7

"OKAY, LET'S NOT PANIC YET," SAID EM NERVOUSLY. SHE began to pace. "Let's think this through."

But Zarya had already figured it out. "I was in the light!" she exclaimed. "I was in front of the footlights, and we got distracted by the accident, and she never turned them off! They took my magic, but I never got it back!"

Em brightened. "Okay! Okay, that makes sense. So your magic is still in the lights, and we just have to go get it."

Arkayna put her hands on her hips. "How could she have forgotten to turn them off? That's so careless!"

"Or maaaaaaaybe," Piper chimed in, "she did it on purpose, because she didn't want you to have magic anymore!"

"Hey!" Zarya flung a hand out toward Piper. "Stop that. She wouldn't do that, and besides, I never even told her I *have* magic."

"But maybe she suspected somehow," said Arkayna, nodding. "She told you her family made her feel bad for not being magical; maybe this is a trick she plays on people to even the score. Or maybe she was just mad that you turned down her offer."

"Or *maybe* it was just an accident!" Zarya said.

Em and Choko jumped in between the others. Choko began waving his paws in "calm down" motions and cheeping soothingly.

"Look, no need to jump to conclusions," said Em. "Let's just go to her truck, ask her what happened, and get the magic back. Easy, right?"

Zarya pointed at Em. "See? She agrees with me. We're going to sort this out in, like, ten minutes. You'll see."

Ten minutes later, the three Mysticons and Zarya, wearing a hooded cloak to hide her face, landed in the small field and jumped off their griffins.

"You still think this is going to be easy?" Arkayna said, motioning around her at the empty grass.

Amileth's truck was gone.

Em winced. "Okay, I have to admit, this doesn't look great."

"I *knew* she was tricky!" Piper blurted. "Oooh, I wish we knew where she was going!"

Arkayna pointed at the ground, where the truck's wheels had left fresh ruts as it drove off. "These are pretty deep tracks. I bet if we follow them we'll catch up with her. No way that truck is as fast as our griffins."

"Yeah, we'll catch her, and we'll *make* her give the magic back!" said Piper, shaking her fist in the air. "No one steals from my best friend!"

"Whoa, whoa, whoa, everyone stop!" Zarya stared at the other girls in disbelief. "I can't believe you're turning on her like this. You don't know *anything* for sure; you just want to think she's bad somehow. Especially you," she finished, rounding on Arkayna.

"Why would I want that?" asked Arkayna.

"Because you're jealous, obviously!" Zarya said. "You're jealous that I like her, and that she's smart and funny and we have more in common than you and I do, and none of that is her problem, it's *yours*."

Arkayna gasped.

"Arrrrrgh!" Zarya tipped her head back and growled in frustration, trying to get ahold of herself. "Listen, I didn't mean it to come out like that. I'm just . . . you're all ready to assume she's evil or something, and that's weird! So here's what we're going to do. I know where she's going, and *I'm* going to go find her. By myself."

"Uh, Zarya, I'm not sure that's the best idea," stammered Em.

"Yeah, Z!" Piper added. "We're a team!"

"We are a team," Zarya replied, "but this doesn't *need* a team. I'm just gonna go talk to her, and we'll fix this, and then I'll be back. Besides, her house sounded pretty private, and she only invited me."

"She only invited you to visit her truck, too, and look how that turned out," said Arkayna. "I am not letting you go on your own!"

Zarya raised her eyebrows. "*Letting* me?"

Arkayna either didn't hear Zarya's warning tone, or didn't care. "Besides," she went on, "now you don't even have your powers. What are you going to do without us if something goes wrong?"

"Oh, so now I can't even take care of myself?" Zarya spun on her heel and marched toward her griffin. "This is ridiculous. Come on, Archer." She sprang up on the griffin's back, and with a powerful leap, Archer took to the air.

"Zarya, come back!" Arkayna yelled, running for her own griffin. "You know I didn't mean that!"

To herself, Zarya huffed, "I'm not so sure." She watched as the other three Mysticons mounted their griffins and flew after her. "So it's gonna be like that, huh? Come on, boy, let's lose 'em."

Zarya turned Archer toward the busiest part of Drake City. They banked and swooped between skyscrapers, heading for the twisty passages of the Undercity.

Zarya finally flew Archer down low and landed in an out-of-the-way back alley. In seconds, she had convinced a friendly dumpster she knew to let her and Archer hide behind it. The dumpster opened its mouth wide, its upper jaw tipping up to cover their heads. A minute later, the Mysticons soared by overhead, and Zarya nodded in grim satisfaction.

"Nice work, buddy, thanks," she told the dumpster. Then she patted Archer's flank. "Let's get going."

She mounted up, and she and Archer flew for the Weaving Woods. *I'm on my own, and that's what I wanted,* she thought as they traveled. *Definitely. My stomach hurts for some other reason. Maybe I'm hungry. This was a good plan.* Then she sighed. What she really wanted, badly, was to be right.

In Which Everyone
Gets Nowhere

8

A LONG FLIGHT LATER, ARCHER BANKED IN LOW CIRCLES OVER what, as far as Zarya could tell, was the center of the Weaving Woods. The moon shone brightly overhead, and Wells's Comet was now easy to pick out in the night sky; it was visibly larger than the other stars and twinkled dramatically as it continued to approach Drake City.

Below Zarya and Archer, things were a lot less clear. The trees for which the woods were named stretched in an unbroken tapestry, growing so densely at their tops that the branches wove themselves together. It was impossible to see anything below the canopy, and there was no safe place to land anywhere near where Zarya wanted to go.

"Well, it wouldn't be much of a challenge if we could just drop right on top of the house, I guess," Zarya said. "Come on, Archer. I think we flew over a clearing back there."

The griffin wheeled around, and soon they found a space big enough for him to land in. Touching down, Archer chuffed in dissatisfaction as his feet sank into the muddy ground.

"Yuck, sorry." Zarya patted his feathery flank as she peered into the trees. A small path led in the direction she wanted to go, but it was barely wide enough for her. "I think I'm gonna have to take it from here. You head home and get cleaned up, okay?"

Archer squawked in concern as she slid down his side and squelched into the mud.

"Hey, not you, too," said Zarya sternly. "I'll be okay, you big softie."

Zarya's phone chirped. It was maybe the twentieth glyph the girls had sent her since she set out, and the noise was starting to get on her nerves. She looked down. The message from Piper read *plzzzzzz where r u. look Choko is sad!* In the accompanying picture, Piper's fingers were pulling the corners of Choko's mouth down in an exaggerated grimace.

Archer tipped his head to the side, staring at her phone.

"Oh yeah, good idea." Zarya quickly typed a glyph to the other girls. *Archer on his way back. I am good. Back soon. STOP WORRYING.* "Okay, now they won't panic when you show up by yourself."

Butting his beak up against her shoulder, Archer gave one last squawk and then took to the air. Zarya watched as he flapped out of sight.

Bee-doop! A glyph came in from Piper, followed by *bee-doop bee-doop bee-doop*: one from Em and two from Arkayna in rapid succession. Zarya sighed. "They really need to chill out," she muttered as she squished through the mud and out of the clearing.

They did not chill out. After an hour and what she estimated was at least a zillion glyphs, calls, and chat requests, Zarya was feeling less than calm herself. The moon shone through a thousand gaps in the leafy canopy, which meant

Zarya could see exactly how dirty her boots were getting as she stomped along the muddy trail. The path twisted and turned and split, but there was always a fork that seemed to be going toward the center of the forest. Now, though, as Zarya stood at the latest fork, peering left and right into the gloom, she could swear she had just been here. Maybe more than once.

She looked at the trees around her and thought for a moment. Then, reaching into the dense underbrush that crowded the path, she pulled out a fallen branch bent in an L-shape. She placed the branch carefully on the path so that the leafy side pointed back the way she had come and the sharp, broken bit pointed down the right-hand fork.

Arrows, she thought, admiring her handiwork. *Always useful.* Then she headed down the right path. At the next fork she made another arrow and took the right-hand path again. And again. And again, until she lost count.

She was trudging along, dismissing another round of glyph notifications on her phone, when her foot hit something. In front of her was another fork, and under her foot, unmistakable in the mud, was her first makeshift arrow. She was going in circles.

Bee-doop! went her phone.

"Arrrrgh, that is *enough*!" Zarya burst out. "Enough of *you*," she said to her phone, silencing it and shoving it deep in her pocket. Then she bent and picked up the branch. "And enough of *this*!" In her frustration, she hurled it off the path and into the woods on the left.

Crack. Midflight, the branch changed direction and fell to the ground.

"What the hex?" muttered Zarya. She stepped to the edge of the path and peered into the dim forest. As far as she could tell, there was nothing between the trees. But the arrow had definitely hit something. She looked more closely at the underbrush in front of her. It was thick, and there were more than a few bugburs. Zarya sighed. She needed to know.

Carefully, she stepped off the path and picked her way toward where the branch had fallen. Arms out to either side for balance, staring at her feet, she was totally unprepared when she slammed forehead-first into the mirror.

*In Which Zarya Reflects
on Many Things*

9

"OW," ZARYA YELPED, HER HAND GOING TO HER HEAD. WITH her other hand, she reached ahead of her and splayed her fingers across the mirror, looking up and around to check for edges. She had to admit, it was very clever.

The mirror was mounted between two of the closely set trees at a sharp angle to the path, and it went up much higher than Zarya's head. She walked along the mirror to the tree on its right and reached out again; sure enough, another mirror was set at a complementary, opposite angle, filling the gap between the next two trees. Glancing over her shoulder at the path and then back, Zarya confirmed her suspicion: The mirrors reflected the trees back on themselves, and the angle made the deception invisible to anyone on the path.

"I'm in a maze," she realized. Then she smirked. "And I know just how to get out of it."

She looked up. The lowest branch on the tree in front of her was ten feet up, but that didn't stop Zarya. Grabbing hold of the knobs on the trunk and cramming her feet into the wedge between the mirror and the tree, she shimmied up. Swinging a leg over the branch, she braced her hands in front of her on the trunk and looked around.

At what was now the level of her waist, the mirrors ended. Their silvered tops glinted in the moonlight in jagged lines, zigging back and forth as they stretched away from her in branches, forks, and switchbacks. This, Zarya realized, was the part of the maze she would have been lost in if she had taken any of the left-hand turns.

"But the right forks all led me in a circle," she murmured. "So what's in the middle of the circle?" She scooched around on the branch until she could see behind her.

It was a house. And even though it was still a little ways off, and even though some of it was still blocked by the trees, Zarya knew it was the strangest house she'd ever seen. The part on the first floor, roughly in the middle, looked more or less like a regular cottage. But oddly shaped rooms and wings and balconies and towers had been stuck on wherever they would fit, in different styles, bending around trees and at one point bridging a small creek, until the whole thing was a huge, ramshackle structure. The tallest point, an elongated pyramid perched on a three-story-high clapboard tower on the left side, ended just below the tree canopy. And as best Zarya could make out in the dim light, all of the various styles of roof, all over the house, were painted green.

No wonder Archer and I couldn't find it from the air, she thought, grinning. Then another thought hit her, and she peered into the trees again. *I wonder if Ami has cameras set up. I bet I looked pretty dumb walking in circles out here. Oh, hey: I wonder if she times people to see how fast they can make it through!* Zarya's grin sharpened as she slid down to the ground.

Quickly, she ran across the path and into the brush on the opposite side, cursing as the thorns snagged her pants. In less than a minute she had scaled a tree, swung her legs over a mirror wall, and dropped down outside the maze.

On this side, the underbrush was much less thick, and the bugburs disappeared entirely. Zarya jogged toward the house, already planning what she would say when Ami swung the door open. She felt like she had definitely figured out the maze faster than most people would have. Maybe she should play it humble: "Sorry it took me so long"? *Nah, that's lame,* Zarya thought, scolding herself as she mounted the steps to the porch. *You can do better than that. Think, girl, think.* She stepped onto the welcome mat and reached for the doorbell, then stopped short.

The shiny silver doorbell wasn't real. It was just painted on. Zarya leaned closer. The brass doorknob was paint, too, just a flat decoration on the wood of the door. Or, more accurately, on the wood of the house; the whole door was a fake.

There was no way in.

In Which Zarya's Mind Is Sharp,
but Something Sharper Awaits

10

ZARYA CHUCKLED. *SHOULD HAVE KNOWN IT WOULDN'T BE that easy,* she thought. She stepped back, away from the house, her eyes crawling over the exterior, looking for clues. Above the gabled roof of the porch, a window on the second story caught her attention. It looked like its bottom half was slightly raised, and its glass panes glinted in the moonlight, so it definitely wasn't painted on.

Zarya climbed onto the wooden porch railing, reached high, and boosted herself up to the low overhang. She put a hand out toward the window but immediately drew it back, shaking her head in amusement. The window glass and frame were real, yes. But they were mounted directly onto a blank, unbroken wall, painted black to look like a dark room beyond.

After jumping back down, Zarya did a quick survey of a few more windows on ground level. The first few she tried were like the one above the porch: real windows, mounted over paintings of black rooms or drawn curtains. She felt a brief surge of elation when the fourth window actually opened onto an interior space, but it was just a small, isolated storage room with no access deeper into the house. Idly, she lifted the lid of a crate in the storage room and laughed out loud; it was full of more window frames.

I'm being too obvious, Zarya thought. *And I'm acting like a thief, crawling in windows and stuff. This isn't right.* She climbed out of the storage room and approached the porch again. *I'm an invited guest, so how would Ami want invited guests to think? She did say I was welcome anyt—Hey.*

Zarya bent down and examined the blue mat in front of the painted-on door. WELCOME was written across it in bold black letters. She tugged on one corner of the mat, but it was tightly attached to the porch. Bending back the stiff fibers at the mat's edge, though, she could see a definite crack in the floorboards below.

This has gotta be it! thought Zarya. *It's a trapdoor!* She scrabbled all around the edges of the mat, looking for a way to open it, but nothing budged. Sitting back on her heels and staring into space, thinking, she found herself looking at the doorbell again. It was definitely painted on, and fairly cartoonishly, now that she was up close to it. But . . .

Stepping closer and leaning way in, so her nose almost brushed the paint, Zarya squinted. Right along the edges of the round bell, she could see the faintest of cracks, almost as if the circle actually pressed in a bit. She shrugged. "Why not?" she muttered, and pushed on the fake doorbell.

The painted wood gave slightly, but nothing happened. Zarya realized she had been holding her breath, and she let it out in a disappointed huff. *Bugbears, I really thought I had it.* She allowed herself a small stamp of frustration, which was muffled by the fiber of the mat.

Whoa, hold up, she thought, eyes widening. *I'm standing on the mat. What if I . . .* She hopped to one side of the mat and, stretching her arm out, pressed the "bell" again.

This time the whole welcome mat popped up—its back edge acting like a hinge—and swung open, banging to a stop against the fake front door. The underside of the mat was bright yellow, with a black winky face on it. Peering into the newly revealed hole in the porch, Zarya saw the first few rungs of a ladder, stretching down into the darkness under the house.

"Nice one, Ami," said Zarya. Still trying to think of what she'd say to the illusionist first when she saw her, she clambered down the ladder.

But at the bottom, her words dried up again. She was in a huge, dimly lit basement. The basement was one big room, and it was fully furnished; Zarya could make out a couple of couches and a few sets of tables and chairs. Overlapping woven rugs covered the floor, and posters from Ami's tours around the world were framed and hung on the walls. Maybe at one point this had been a living room or a game room. But around and on top of the furniture were all kinds of props and memorabilia, stacked up everywhere and making the large room feel cramped and cluttered. It looked a bit like the inside of Ami's truck, with two differences: Everything was stacked haphazardly in the open instead of being organized into crates, and everything looked . . . Zarya couldn't quite put her finger on it . . .

"Abandoned," she finally muttered. That was it. In the truck, Ami had clearly been working on everything, tinkering and perfecting. But here were the tricks that she was finished with, or that never worked. An iron tank, an elaborate clockwork dollhouse, fruit made of marble and flowers made of wood, and on and on. Here were the trinkets picked up in her travels, snow globes and ornaments and sculptures and novelty hats, that she had no use for, the kind that were displayed proudly for a year or two and then tossed aside.

Standing amid the castoffs of Ami's life, Zarya felt a surge of discomfort. A few hours ago in Ami's truck, Zarya had felt a real connection to the illusionist. But their lives were so different. While Zarya was running cons for small change in the Undercity, Ami had been traveling the world. How many places had Ami been that Zarya had never even heard of?

Maybe we don't have so much in common after all, Zarya thought. Then she shook herself. *Stop talking yourself out of things, Z.* She had hung out with Ami, and she liked Ami, and she was pretty sure Ami liked her, too. That was enough.

With new resolve, Zarya strode across the basement and around a corner, where she found a set of stairs leading up. Still lost in thought, she put a foot on the first step . . . then yanked it back as a huge sword came swinging at her out of the wall.

Shhhhing! Shing! Shing! One after another, curved blades sliced down from hidden grooves in the walls and ceiling and began swinging back and forth over the steps. Zarya's eyes widened as, within seconds, twenty blades blocked her path to the top of the stairs. There was no break in the pattern, no safe way to dart by.

She was stuck.

In Which There Are Bolts from the Blue

11

ZARYA'S MIND RACED. *AMI COMES DOWN HERE A LOT TO DROP stuff off,* she thought. *Think like her. I know I wouldn't want to have to deal with a sword storm every time I put something away. So there must be an easy way to turn it off.*

Zarya poked around at the bottom of the stairs for a few minutes, looking for a switch, a lever, a button. Anything to stop the blades, which continued to swoosh back and forth. Then she sighed. *Ami doesn't live down here, genius,* she berated herself. *There* is *an easy way to turn this trap off. And it's at the top of the stairs.*

But Zarya knew there must be some way past from

this side. *What, she invited me all this way just for me to get stuck in the basement? Nah. There's gotta be something. . . .* She went back to studying the blades. *Say Ami comes in through the trapdoor sometimes. She's not gonna do an acrobatics routine through these knives, jumping around like Piper when she's had too much sugar, just to get up to the bathroom. That's not her style. And why risk getting cut at all?*

Hey, maybe that's it!

Zarya reached into her pocket and pulled out the piece of parchment Ami had given her. Gingerly, she held it out over the bottom step.

Slice! On its next pass, the first blade chopped the paper neatly in two. Zarya dropped the half still in her hand with a muffled yelp. "Okay," she breathed. "Definitely real blades. Definitely real, *sharp* blades."

Then she replayed what she had just said. *I'm assuming too much,* she realized. *There is definitely* one *real blade. That's all I know for sure.* She peered closely at the rest of the blades. It was hard to tell since they were moving, but were they less shiny than the first one? And was there something slightly less . . . swoopy about the way they were swooping?

She looked around at the nearby stacks of memorabilia. She didn't want to risk wrecking anything sentimental or valuable, but . . . there. Balanced on the top of one pile was a familiar sight—a cheap, plastic novelty wand with MAGI MALL written down its length. Zarya snatched it up and returned to the bottom of the stairs.

Waiting for the first blade to pass again, she took a deep breath. "Ugh, I hope I'm right about this," she said. "And if I'm not, Ami, I'll buy you a new wand." *Swish.* The sharp blade swung past. Zarya stretched her arm forward over the bottom steps, thrusting the wand directly into the path of the second blade.

Clunk. The blade hit the wand and rebounded backward, juddering to a halt. This second sword wasn't sharp, and it weighed almost nothing at all!

"Yesssss!" Zarya hissed in triumph. Then she remembered the danger and snatched her arm back—barely in time. She felt the breeze of the sharp first blade on her fingertips.

But now she knew the secret. Jumping to the safe space where the second blade had swung, she stuck the wand out to intersect the third blade. *Clunk.* Another fake. Stepping up again, she checked the fourth blade.

Clunk. And the fifth. *Clunk.* She was starting to chuckle, but she had to check each one just to be sure. *Clunk.* *Clunk. Clunk.* Zarya worked her way up the stairs, leaving a trail of blunt, hollow swords dangling behind her.

At the top of the steps, she swung the door wide, a triumphant smile on her face, half expecting Ami to be there waiting for her. But there was no one . . . and nothing. She was standing at the bottom of a wide, tall, nearly empty silo. A spiral staircase, its railing decorated with strings of white lights, wound around the inside wall of the space to a hatch in the ceiling about forty feet up. Long metal poles and planks of wood leaned against the wall near the door she had just come through, and paint spattered the floor.

Zarya realized she was standing in the tower she had noticed from the outside, the one topped by the pyramid. She crossed the room to the paint splatters. Clearly, something huge had been laid out on the floor in here. Zarya raised her eyebrows as she had a thought. *Did Ami build this room 'cause she needed a space to work out one of her tricks? Were all the strange rooms I saw from the outside built the way they were so specific tricks could fit inside them? Does Ami think of an illusion and then design the*

87

perfect room to make it in? Zarya shook her head. *That's weird . . . but pretty great, actually.*

FWOOM. Zarya's head snapped up, her train of thought broken. That sounded like an explosion, and it came from the room right above her. Quickly she crossed to the steps and bounded up them.

FWOOM again, followed by *CRASH.* Something was definitely going on up there. Maybe Ami was in trouble! Zarya took stock as she sprinted up the last few stairs. She had no powers, sure. But she was still *her,* and she could outsmart anyone dumb enough to mess with her friend.

Zarya reached the hatch and pushed it open a few inches, peeking cautiously through. She could see Ami's booted feet a little ways in front of her, facing something deeper in the room. From what Zarya could tell, Ami's feet were in a ready stance, her right foot back and braced against the floor.

Carefully, Zarya pushed the hatch open another inch, just in time to see a flash of blue light, accompanied by another *FWOOM.* Was Ami being attacked? Or was she attacking someone else with some kind of energy weapon? Running out of patience, Zarya shoved the hatch open and stuck her head all the way through.

Then she froze. She was near one corner of the inside of a pyramid that went up about fifty feet, and it was as full as the room below had been empty. A complex system of pulleys, ropes, winches, bars, and moving platforms filled the narrowing space above. Curtains, like the ones Ami used in her act, were hung from some of the bars, while others held reflective panels and others supported stage lights. A row of seats was set up against the wall next to Zarya's head, and a bank of control panels stretched away down the wall in front of her. Spare curtains, parts of lights, strangely shaped mirrors, and other odds and ends were scattered around the room, resting on the empty seats and piled against the walls. Zarya figured this was how Ami tested the sight lines for her stage act, to make sure the mechanisms for her tricks stayed safely invisible.

Right now, Ami was the only other person in the room. She was wearing her full stage outfit, facing bottles of fizzy star water dangling from ropes in the middle of the room. As Zarya watched, Ami raised her hand and concentrated.

FWOOM. A bolt of blue energy shot out of Ami's hand and smashed into the bottle on the left. It exploded, pieces clinking to the ground to join a growing pile of broken glass.

Ami nodded, then muttered, "Okay, but what if I . . ." She raised her hand again.

SHWIP. This time a coil of blue light extended from her hand, unraveling across the room to loop around the bottle. Ami jerked her hand backward and the loop tightened, cracking the bottle in half.

This time Ami laughed out loud. "Now *this* is amazing," she said.

Zarya stared. It wasn't shaped like a bow and arrows, but she would know that blue energy anywhere. Arkayna, Piper, Em—they were all right. And Zarya was so, so wrong.

Amileth had stolen Zarya's magic.

In Which Zarya Throws Shade
(and Several Other Things)

12

ZARYA'S FACE FELT HOT, AND HER HANDS SHOOK. SHE FELT sick. No, she felt angry.

No, that wasn't it, either. Well, it was part of it, but not all of it.

She felt *embarrassed*.

Here she was, jumping through hoops to find someone she had just met, wondering if she needed to hurry to make a good impression, planning out what she was going to say. And the whole time Ami had been here, playing with Zarya's stolen power.

On top of all that, Zarya had ditched her *real* friends,

and had gotten mad at them for telling her what was *clearly* the truth. How was she going to face them? What was she going to say to Arkayna? When she thought about what she *had* said to Arkayna . . .

SKKKKSSSSH. Zarya snapped back to the present as Ami whipped her hand from left to right, sending out a barrage of blue energy spikes that smashed one bottle after another.

"*Enough,*" Zarya snarled. Her hands clenched, and she looked down in surprise to see that she was still holding the plastic wand. Without thinking, she pulled back her fist and hurled the wand toward the nearest control panel.

The plastic clanked against a switch, flipping it to the side, and Ami leapt back in surprise as the long pipe holding up the bottles rocketed toward the ground with a clatter. Then the illusionist whirled around to face Zarya.

"Oh! You—you got here so fast!" the elf girl stammered.

A part of Zarya's mind noted that, in another context, this was exactly the reaction she had been hoping for. But all that was ruined now.

"You didn't think I'd come looking for my magic?"

challenged Zarya. Warily, she began edging toward the controls.

"Of course I did, I just thought . . ." Ami raised her hands to her head and looked distraught.

Zarya narrowed her eyes. "So you *did* know! You did this on purpose!"

"No! I mean, yes, I knew it was yours, but . . ." Ami reached a hand out. "Zarya, I swear, I—"

"Keep your hands down," Zarya hissed, ducking.

Ami froze, shocked. "Zarya, I'm not going to . . . Just *listen.*" She dropped her hand and took a step forward.

"Stop." Zarya put a hand up in warning. With the other, she groped along the wall beside her for the nearest bank of controls.

"Wait, don't touch those," Ami said, a new tension in her voice. "You don't know what they are."

"I don't know what *you* are." Zarya's hand came to rest on a large lever.

"That's not fair!" Ami retorted. Zarya watched in alarm as her eyes began to flicker with blue sparks. Ami raised a hand, finger pointed accusingly at Zarya. Were those blue sparks on her fingertips?

Panicking, Zarya shoved the lever down. Ropes attached to one side of a wooden platform, suspended halfway up the far wall, went slack, and the platform swung down toward Amileth.

Ami spun and thrust her hands out, and a sheet of crackling blue light shot from her splayed fingertips. The platform smashed into the blue energy, the force of it shoving Ami back a few inches. The sheet of blue cracked apart and dissolved, but it had done its job. Ami spun to face Zarya again, her eyes now fully glowing blue.

Zarya reached for the next lever.

"*Don't*," warned Ami. Her clenched fists glowed.

I have to keep her off-balance, Zarya thought. *Keep her from attacking me.* She pulled the lever.

A heavy metal pulley dropped from the top of the room, right toward Ami's head. But again, Ami was ready. She swung a hand, and a blue bolt caught the pulley in mid-drop, sending it careening into a tangle of ropes.

"*Stop it*," Ami demanded, stomping toward Zarya. "Why are you doing this?"

"Why am *I* doing this?" Zarya almost laughed as she reached for the next lever. "Look at *you!*"

"Look at . . ." Ami repeated, glancing down at her hands. She saw the crackles of blue and stopped dead. "Oh." Then she caught a glimpse of herself in a nearby mirror, and her glowing blue eyes went wide. *"OH."*

Immediately she backed away from Zarya, hands falling to her sides. The light in her eyes went out, replaced by a look of alarm. "I didn't know. Zarya, I didn't know. Why would I attack you," she continued, and now she looked imploring, "when I have so many questions?"

In Which Everything Comes
So Close to Going Right

13

ZARYA KEPT HER HAND ON THE LEVER. "YOU . . . DIDN'T KNOW you were shooting scary sparks out of your eyes?"

"*No,*" said Ami emphatically. "How would I? This is all totally new to me!"

"And totally *mine.*"

"I know." Ami slumped to her knees, her shoulders falling. "I mean, I know *now.* I didn't turn the footlights off for a while after you'd left, and then . . . well, there was a hum, so I knew *something* had been stored in there, but I didn't know what it was. And I didn't expect it to go into *me.*" She looked up, a hint of accusation in her eyes. "You didn't tell me you had magic!"

Chagrined, Zarya finally let her hand fall. "It's not something I'm supposed to talk about," she admitted. "And, for the record, I don't use it to make angry eye sparks."

Ami chuckled. "Fair enough. So what *do* you use it for?" Seeing Zarya's hesitation, she shrugged. "*I've* told *you* quite a few secrets tonight. And besides, if you tell me, it might help me figure out how to get the magic back into you."

Zarya gasped. She wasn't even sure where to start. "First of all," she said after a moment of sputtering. "You don't know how to give my magic *back*?!"

"This has never happened before!" Ami protested. "I have some ideas we could try, though."

"I bet you do. But, okay, you do *want* to give it back, right?"

"Of course I do!"

"Then why didn't you come find me right away?" Zarya demanded.

It was Ami's turn to hesitate. "I, um," she started. She took a deep breath and tried again. "You have to understand. I always wondered what it would be like to have magic. And I thought, well . . . I don't know what you use the power for, so I hoped you wouldn't notice for a few hours. I was going to experiment tonight and then track you down in the morning. You're the princess. I figured you wouldn't be hard to find." Ami's eyes brightened. "Oh, I didn't think of that until just now. Does magic run in your family? Does Princess Arkayna have it, too?"

Zarya squirmed. "It's not . . . that kind of magic."

Ami leaned forward eagerly. "What do you mean? What kind is it?"

"It's . . . uh, well, you were experimenting with it. What do you think?"

Letting out a laugh, Ami got to her feet. "Smooth deflection, Princess."

Zarya blushed. Ami motioned her closer, and she went to stand with the illusionist in the middle of the room.

"Watch this," Ami said. She held up a hand, and a thin blue rope of energy unfurled from one finger. She made a lashing motion, and the energy whipped toward a control panel, neatly pressing one button. Above them, a stage light went out.

"The whip is pretty cool, sure," Zarya said.

"Wait." Ami closed her fist, dissipating the energy. Zarya watched as Ami opened her hand again, but this time nothing happened.

"Still getting the hang of—" Zarya teased. But her quip dried up as Ami made another lashing motion with her empty hand, and across the room Zarya heard the *click* of the same button as before. She squinted as the stage light came back on. "Whooooooooa," she whispered, impressed. "How did you—"

"I have *no idea*," Ami said. "But I can decide whether or not the whip is visible. Do you know what this means for the act?"

"Wait, the act? What does this have to do with the act?" Zarya took a wary step away from her. "I thought you wanted to give the magic back."

Ami nodded enthusiastically. "I do! I will! But then you should *definitely* come with me! I already knew we would make a good team, but now? Zarya, with my craftsmanship and your magic, we will be the greatest show in Gemina!"

Zarya relaxed, letting her breath out in relief. Then she shook her head sadly. "Ami, I can't. I have this . . . it's sort of a job, I guess. It means a lot to me, and I can't just walk away from it."

"What, being a princess? Your sister has all the princess duties covered, I can tell. Take a vacation! Make a career change!" Impulsively, Ami grabbed Zarya's hands and pulled her closer. *"Come with me."*

Zarya opened her mouth to explain everything. To tell Ami that she was a Mysticon, to explain that it was much more than a job, that she was part of an unbreakable team—a sisterhood—bound together by duty and loyalty and friendship and family and magic, all at once. But she never got the chance.

KA-KRAAAACK! With a huge rending of wood and metal, the top of the pyramid lifted off and toppled away. Zarya and Ami threw their hands up to shield themselves as splinters of wood and coils of rope fell all around them.

Squinting up through the settling debris, Zarya saw that something had bent back the trees all around the house, giving a clear view of the night sky. Hovering in the sky were three familiar figures, mounted on griffins.

No, Zarya thought. *Oh, NO.*

"AMILETH," came Arkayna's voice, booming from above in full Dragon Mage mode. *"RELEASE THE PRINCESS AND RETURN WHAT YOU HAVE STOLEN."*

In Which a Rescue Turns Regrettable and
a Friend Turns Foe

14

STILL CROUCHED DEFENSIVELY, AMILETH STARED AT THE
Dragon Mage, stunned. "The Mysticons?" She blinked.
"*Most* of the Mysticons. But how did you . . . and why
would you . . ." She gasped and turned to Zarya. "*You.* This
is what you were talking about."

Zarya nodded miserably. "I was about to tell—"

Amileth kept talking. "*This* is your job? You're a
Mysticon? But I heard the Mysticons were heroes!"

"You heard right, lady!" yelled Piper. "So give that
magic back already!"

Straightening, Amileth threw her shoulders back

and addressed the airborne girls. "You come here unin-vited," she began. "You invade my privacy and destroy my home. And you accuse me of, what, holding Zarya against her will, without a hint of proof?" Her eyes began to glow and crackle, and her lip turned up in a sneer. "These are not the actions of *heroes*. How *dare* you!"

"Ami, wait!" Zarya jumped in front of Amileth and put a hand on her shoulder. "This is all a mistake!" Then she turned to Arkayna. "Why are you here? I told you not to come! How did you even find me?"

Em spoke up. "When you stopped answering glyphs we . . . well, we got worried. Malvaron helped us find a spell to track your phone." She winced. "It seemed like a great idea an hour ago."

Zarya groaned. "I *told* you not to worry! So many times!"

"But we *did*," said Arkayna. "And we were right to! You're out here with no powers and no backup, facing— well, facing *her*!" She gestured to Amileth, who gri-maced.

Zarya clenched her fists. "I wasn't *facing*—"

"No, Princess, the Dragon Mage is right," said Ami, stepping away. "You came here ready for a fight."

"I didn't!" Zarya protested. "But when I saw you had my powers, I—"

"You knew the rest of your team was looking for you," Ami continued, her hands tightening into fists, "and you left your phone on, which means you *let* them track you here. Was this your plan, to stall me until they arrived?"

"Probably!" Piper called out. "She's really good at plans!"

Zarya waved her hands frantically at Piper, groping for words. "I—no—"

"Normally," Ami said, so softly that only Zarya could hear, "I would really like that about you." She gestured, and the blue light uncoiled from her fingers and hissed against the ground.

"Izzie, go!" cried Arkayna, urging her griffin into a dive. She waved her staff, and a green energy blast shot from the orb and impacted at Ami's feet, making the illusionist jump back. In the same motion, Arkayna leapt into the air and landed nimbly in front of Ami, her staff held out protectively to block Ami's access to Zarya. "If you want to get to her," Arkayna said, "you come through me." She pointed an imperious finger at Ami. "Now: Give. That. Magic. Back."

"STOP," Zarya screamed, startling everyone. She balled

up her fists at her temples. "You've got it all wrong!" she yelled at Arkayna. "All of it! She didn't do this on purpose, and *I* can take care of myself, and *you* are ruining *everything*!"

Ami tilted her head to the side. "It's a good show, Princess," she said, "but after all this, I don't think I'm buying it."

Zarya opened her mouth to say something, anything. "Ami, I—"

But Ami thrust her hands out, and blue, sparkling smoke came pouring from her fingertips.

"Don't let her get away!" Arkayna commanded, stepping forward.

"You're still not *listening*," howled Zarya desperately.

In seconds, the smoke surrounded all four Mysticons. They couldn't see one another, let alone Amileth.

"Uh, I don't think the Striker and I can land in this," said Em.

From the corner of the room came a *bang* and then a ratcheting *clank*.

"What's that?" yelped Piper.

"It's the way out of here, locking behind her," said Zarya. "Ami's gone."

In Which the Escaping Entertainer
Encounters a Familiar Face

15

AMI BOLTED DOWN THE SPIRAL STAIRS, THROUGH THE DOOR to the basement, and down the steps past the dangling swords. Her heart was racing and her hands were sweating. Weaving her way expertly between the piles of trinkets and props, she approached a large framed poster on the wall. The poster showed a grinning Ami, loops of heavy chain restraining her from neck to toes, under the headline *The Amazing Amileth and Her Extraordinary Escapes!*

Ami ran a hand along the underside of the ornate frame and pressed a catch. Silently, the poster and its glass swung back, revealing a secret passage. She swung her legs over the lip of the frame and groped along the tunnel wall for the flashlight she kept there.

Then she stopped and her lips quirked. She snapped her fingers, and a blue flame appeared, hovering before her. Nodding in satisfaction, she hurried down the tunnel.

Several twists and turns and one long staircase later, she reached the hidden garage where her truck was waiting. She hauled herself up into the cab, started the engine, and floored the accelerator.

Speeding along her underground driveway, which would take her to a secluded back road just outside the Weaving Woods, Ami finally had a chance to think.

What just happened? And what do I do now? She didn't have a good answer to either question. Her perfectly designed, wonderfully useful house was damaged and compromised, perhaps forever. She needed to act as if the contents of this truck were all she had left in the world.

She felt another surge of anger toward the Mysticons. She had done *nothing* wrong. She had accidentally borrowed something that she fully intended to give back, and look what they had done in return! And Zarya, especially—to think that Ami had felt a connection with her, had thought they shared so much in common, and had assumed Zarya had felt the same. Ami's brow furrowed. Zarya was just another spoiled princess, throwing a tantrum when she couldn't immediately get her way. Well, she was just going to have to live with disappointment.

Ami huffed in frustration as the truck chugged up a steep incline toward the surface. What *was* she going to do now? The Mysticons would hunt her down, and when they found her they would—what? Ami honestly didn't know, and she didn't want to find out.

She couldn't believe that those four girls were the revered, chosen Mysticons. She had heard such glowing things about them—how they had saved Drake City time and time again, from orcs and the undead and evil liches and who knew what else. And the people of the city loved them for it, apparently. Ami snorted. What rubes.

Do the Mysticons just keep getting lucky? she wondered as she steered the truck out of the hidden tunnel mouth and onto the road. *Or are they actually fooling—WHOA.*

She slammed on the brakes, hissing air between her

teeth. The huge truck, not made for abrupt stops, juddered alarmingly before coasting to a halt. Six inches from the front bumper, a lone figure stood in the middle of the road. A dark, tattered cape was draped over his broad shoulders, making him almost invisible against the black road. The only thing that stood out clearly, shining in Ami's headlights, was his bare skull, cracked across the top.

It was one of the Mysticons' greatest enemies: Dreadbane.

In Which a Threat Becomes a Plan

16

"THE AMAZING AMILETH," INTONED DREADBANE. HE SPOKE IN
such a low voice, Ami had to strain to hear him over the
truck's idling engine. "I have been looking for you. I followed your vehicle's tracks from the city, but here . . ." He
gestured around him. "They seemed to vanish."

"Yes," said Ami. "That's on purpose."

"It is good you have come to me, then," Dreadbane
said. He didn't move from his place directly in the truck's
path, just continued to stare up at her with his glowing
red eyes.

"Listen," snapped Ami. "On any other night, this

quiet, menacing thing you're doing would be making me very nervous. But tonight?" She jumped out of the truck and stalked toward him, crooking her fingers and making blue lightning dance between them. "I am in *no mood.*"

To her surprise, Dreadbane took one look at her glowing hands and sighed with dismay. "Ah," he said. "I was hoping your show was a genuine marvel, but I see it is not. How disappointing."

"My *show*?" Ami snorted. "You're standing in the road at night, all settings on Maximum Creep, to make me *perform* for you?"

"Not at all. I am not interested in your tricks. I am interested in your footlights. My instincts told me that they actually work to drain away magic, but, since you clearly are a magic user, I conclude that my instincts have failed me. You are a fraud."

"Hey." Ami bristled with pride. "I'm no fraud. The lights work, all right?"

For the first time, Dreadbane's eyes flared with energy. "They work? That is wonderful news." He cleared his throat and raised his voice intimidatingly. "In that case, I am Dreadbane, and I demand that you—"

"As for me being a magic user," Ami went on, oblivious to Dreadbane's demand, "before a few hours ago, I would have been happy about that! Delighted, even! But now? Ha!"

Taken aback, Dreadbane shut his jaw with a snap. After a moment, he lifted a hand in a "go on" gesture.

Ami began to pace back and forth in the road. "I always, *always* thought magic was this wonderful, special thing. Part of me was always sad that I didn't have it. I've spent my whole life imitating it, trying to get close to it. But tonight I finally got it, and right away, things started going wrong. I lost my house. I lost someone I thought was a friend." She flapped her hands, feeling helpless and angry. "It wasn't supposed to be like this!"

Dreadbane nodded. "I agree, Amileth. Magic causes nothing but trouble."

"Exactly!" Ami pointed a finger at him, then continued to pace. "That's exactly what I was getting at."

"So what will you do about it?"

She pulled up short. "*Do* about it?" she echoed.

Dreadbane smiled. It was not a comforting sight, but Ami found herself wanting to listen to him anyway. "You have the power to banish magic from your stage, correct?" he asked. "Why not think bigger?"

"Bigger?" He just kept surprising her. "How do I do that? Do you know how long it took me to build those lights by myself? A stage is about as big as I can manage."

"Ah, but you're not by yourself anymore," replied Dreadbane. "I count two of us here, and I can get more. How big can you think, with an army of helpers at your back?"

Ami's eyes unfocused as she pondered. "I have thought before about building enough lights to perform large-scale illusions. Something that would cover a whole building, or an arena."

Dreadbane leaned toward her. "Bigger. Much bigger. And I'm not talking about a mere illusion. I'm talking about removing the trouble that plagues us both. I am talking about taking magic away . . . from all of Gemina!"

In Which an Outfit Forms
While a Team Unravels

17

"WE CAN FIX THIS," ARKAYNA PLEADED FROM THE DOORWAY to Zarya's room. "Once we catch up to Amileth, we'll—"

"*You* are not catching up to her," shouted Zarya. "You've done enough! I had everything under control, and you . . . you . . . *argh.*" Throwing up her hands, Zarya turned back to her closet in the Stronghold, tossing pants and jackets blindly into the room as she rummaged. Choko, perched on the bed, dodged back and forth to avoid the flying clothes.

The Mysticons had blasted the lock off the pyramid's hatch and searched the rest of the house, but they hadn't found Ami. The ride back to the Stronghold after that was quiet and tense. Zarya had barged straight up to her room, Arkayna on her heels, while Em and Piper had stayed downstairs, looking for a way to track Amileth.

"At least let me help you find what you're looking for in there," Arkayna said now. "Or maybe you can borrow something of mine?"

"I need a disguise," Zarya muttered. "Since I still don't have my magic, and thanks to *you* the person who has it is . . . who even knows where." She flung a belt behind her with one arm, and Choko barely managed to leap over the whirling leather in time.

"We screwed up, I know!" Arkayna said, wringing her hands in distress. "We shouldn't have been so quick to judge her. So let us make it right!"

Zarya rounded on her, a pair of jeans in her hand. "You still don't get it," she said. "Not trusting Ami isn't the only thing you screwed up."

"Okay! Then tell me what else needs fixing, and I'll fix it!"

Zarya tossed the jeans on the bed and stormed across the room, stabbing her finger at Arkayna. "You didn't trust *me*. You don't trust me to be on my own, and you don't trust me to pick my own friends. How are you going to fix *that*?"

"Oh no," Arkayna said. "That's . . . oh, Zarya, that's not what this means at all. I just . . . I love you, so I worry about you, that's all. And sometimes I feel like you don't listen to me when I tell you what I'm worried about."

"Well, you *definitely* don't listen to me when I tell you *not* to worry, so I guess that makes us even."

"I'm so sorry. I really am. But we're a team, Zarya."

"Yeah," snapped Zarya. "A team. Tonight we were a team that found someone powerful and confused and *innocent*, and what did we do? We scared her, smashed up her house, made her mad, and then drove her away." Zarya shook her head. "I don't know if I want to be part of a team like that."

"Zarya!" Arkayna gasped. "What are you saying?"

"Uh, hello?" Em knocked gingerly on the doorframe.

"Em, this isn't the best time," Arkayna said.

Zarya snorted and stuck her head back into her closet.

Em took in the scene and winced sympathetically. "Yeah, I'm super-sorry about that," she replied, "but Nova Terron just sent us a message."

"This isn't the best time for him, either, Em," said

Arkayna. "Zarya and I need to finish talking. We'll get back to him in a minute."

"I hear you," Em said, clearly uncomfortable, "and again, so very sorry. But it can't wait."

Zarya sat back on her heels and looked Em up and down. "Something happened. What happened? Is it Ami?"

"You're not going to believe this, but it's Dreadbane," said Em.

"Yeah!" cried Piper, pushing past Em into the room. "Old Boney's back, and he's in the Sword's Rest graveyard, turning skeletons into . . . well, skeletons! But *alive* ones!"

"He's raising a new army?" said Zarya, jumping to her feet in alarm.

"That's what I said! So let's go!" Piper glanced at the mess on the bed, where Choko had wrapped himself in white and blue fabric and tied a blue sock across his face. She clapped her hands and hugged Zarya. "You're making a costume! You're so smart." Running out of the room, she called over her shoulder, "Hold on, I have a thingy for this!"

Em looked from Zarya to Arkayna, noticing the tension still in the air. She backed out of the room, muttering about getting the griffins ready.

Arkayna fidgeted. "I'm not sure . . . I mean, without your magic, do you . . ." She sighed. "I just want you to be safe!" she blurted.

"Oh, I'm coming with you." Zarya really wanted to find Ami. But Dreadbane was serious business, and she wasn't going to let Arkayna think that she couldn't pull her weight. So she stared Arkayna down, and eventually Arkayna dropped her eyes and left.

Zarya turned to Choko and sighed. "Go, team."

In Which Bones Are Picked

18

AS THE FOUR OF THEM FLEW AT TOP SPEED TOWARD THE graveyard on the outskirts of town, Zarya's eye kept darting to Wells's Comet. Now a quarter as large as the moon, the comet sparkled like a diamond, catching the moonlight and refracting it into thin rays. There were still a few hours until dawn, and Zarya couldn't believe the comet was going to get even closer. *That thing would be scary if it weren't so pretty,* she thought.

She tugged her makeshift cape, hastily constructed from an old sheet, away from her neck. *The magical one doesn't chafe like this,* she thought. *I'm never taking that for granted again.* Absentmindedly, she raised a hand to scratch her cheek.

"Ah ah, no scratching!" Piper sang out as Miss Paisley glided down next to Archer. "You'll smudge your mask *and* get makeup on your glove! Two bads, no goods!"

Zarya dropped her hand with a sigh. That was another thing—her magical mask was way more comfortable. On the other hand, Piper had been so excited to paint the mask on—"Aw, yay, you got some festive face paint after all!" she had squealed—that it almost made up for the itchiness. Almost.

"Eyes front, girls," Arkayna called back. "We're here."

"I see him!" said Em. "Great goblins, he's been busy."

The graveyard stretched in front of them. Paved paths wound among rolling hills, most topped by white stone monuments. Near the center of the graveyard, halfway down one of the larger hills, they could make out Dreadbane, surrounded by at least two dozen white figures. At the bottom of the hill was a huge, animated vulture skeleton, idly pecking the ground as it waited.

Arkayna made a swirling motion with her hand, and the other girls nodded. Together, the griffins banked into a low arc, dropping the Mysticons off silently on the opposite side of the hill. Led by Arkayna, the four of them crept stealthily up the hill and took cover behind the wide monument at its crest.

From here, they had a clear view of Dreadbane holding his hands out over a grave marker. As they watched, he muttered under his breath, tensed his fingers into claws, and raised his hands to the sky. With a low rumble, the gravestone split in two, and a skeleton clawed its way out between the broken halves. At Dreadbane's urging, the skeleton rose to its feet, clutching a longsword in one bony hand. Tattered, batlike wings unfurled from its back, and it screeched at the sky.

"Of course!" Arkayna whispered. "Sword's Rest is where the soldiers were buried after the Battle of Victory Heights!"

"With their weapons and armor," Em put in. "Which doesn't make this easier."

"Ugh," sighed Zarya. "Gotta say, when we beat Necrafa, I was thinking we'd never see this guy again. He seemed so . . ."

"Defeated," finished Arkayna, nodding. "Necrafa broke his heart."

"Looks like he got over it," Zarya said. "Guess he wants to be the big bad now."

"Shushums!" hissed Piper. "I can't hear what he's saying!"

"He's just ordering . . ." Zarya began, but then she trailed off, perking up her ears. That didn't sound like orders.

"Are two spectres for each enough?" Dreadbane was asking.

Zarya frowned. Who was he talking to?

A familiar voice came from a point farther down the hill, past where they could see. "How clever are they? Some pieces will be heavier than others, but maybe it's best to always send three, to make the search faster."

Dreadbane let out a dry chuckle. "My spectres are loyal and fierce, but they are . . . not clever. Three it is." He turned to the next gravestone.

The other girls were all staring at Zarya, who muffled a groan of dismay. The second voice was definitely Ami's!

"What is she—" began Arkayna.

Zarya cut her off with a chopping hand motion. "I don't know. But let's go stop them."

Arkayna nodded and began to stand, then turned back to Zarya. "Just . . ."

"Don't worry," Zarya said confidently. "I'm good." She held up her training bow, still a little dusty from its time in the back of her closet, and patted the quiver of arrows at her hip. "These aren't magic, but they still work for smashing at a distance."

Arkayna gave her an anxious smile. Even though Zarya knew things between them were still unresolved, she felt a wave of warmth toward her sister. It was *killing* Arkayna not to say "be careful" right now, but somehow she was holding it in for Zarya's sake. So Zarya returned the smile, and she was glad to see a little of the tension go out of Arkayna's shoulders.

"Let's go, girls!" announced the Dragon Mage, and the Mysticons sprang into action.

Em tossed a handful of small orbs onto the ground around Dreadbane. Purple, sticky goo boiled up where they landed, covering the grass and gravestones, gluing one skeleton in place halfway out of the dirt, and sticking Dreadbane's feet to the ground. Dreadbane snarled.

"Surprise!" Piper cried out, flinging her three hoops at him. The first one hit right in the center of his forehead, dazing him. The other two caught each of the curved black horns rising from his skull, pulling him backward. With his feet immobilized, Dreadbane pinwheeled his arms for balance but couldn't help collapsing onto his rump. "One thousand points for the Striker!" Piper cheered.

As Dreadbane hacked at the glue with his sword, Arkayna shot green blasts from her staff in quick succession. One by one, the spectres began to fall to the energy blasts.

Seeing this, Dreadbane snarled again. He held his free hand out to a section of graves not covered in goo, raising new spectres as fast as Arkayna could destroy them.

Zarya ran straight down the hill, nocking and firing arrows as she went. The first found its mark in the nearest spectre's skull, and she was turning to find her next target when she realized that the spectre she shot was still moving. *Girl, these normal arrows don't explode*, she reminded herself, loosing two more arrows into the spectre. This time it fell and stayed down. "Ami!" she called. "Ami, what are you doing?"

Ami came into view at the bottom of the hill, a dozen spectres clustered around her. She glanced at Zarya and seemed about to answer her, but then she shook her head and turned back to the spectres. She addressed the three on her left, then turned and gave whispered instructions to the next three.

"You have bigger problems, Ranger!" taunted Dreadbane from behind her. Zarya spun around just in time to dodge a blow from a newly raised spectre carrying a mace. She dropped to the ground and rolled up into a defensive position, but the spectre lost interest in her. Instead, it flapped its wings and glided down to join the growing army around Ami. Zarya looked around and noticed spectre after spectre ignoring the Mysticons and heading for Ami instead.

"I think—" Zarya began, but she was cut off by a warning yelp from Piper. Looking down, she saw another spectre emerging from a grave right at her feet. She danced backward and fired an arrow, pinning the skeleton to the ground. Running back up the hill, she finished her thought: "I think he's trying to stall us!"

Dreadbane laughed. "'Trying'?" He looked down at Ami, who nodded. Tipping his head back, he called to the nearly thirty spectres around her. "You have your orders!" he boomed. "Now *fly!*"

As one, the spectre army rose into the air. Then,

before the Mysticons could launch an attack, the spectres split into ten different groups and flew in ten different directions.

"Form up!" yelled Arkayna. Immediately, Em whistled for the griffins as Arkayna, Zarya, and Piper tried to pick off the retreating spectres. But there were too many, and they were too scattered. Then Zarya heard a rattling, whooshing noise and looked down the hill to see Ami approaching, mounted on the undead vulture.

Arkayna pointed her staff at the vulture.

"You'll hurt Ami!" cried Zarya, reaching out to block Arkayna's shot.

"So sweet, Mysticon," snickered Dreadbane, leaping onto the bird's skeletal neck. "Enjoy your visit to the Sword's Rest." He gestured, and huge bone spikes burst from the ground around the Mysticons and closed over their heads.

It took only a few minutes for the Mysticons to hack themselves free of the cage. But that was enough.

Dreadbane and Ami had escaped.

In Which Spectres Become Collectors

19

as they mounted the griffins. "There are ten squads of
three spectres each descending on the city. We don't know
what they're planning, but it can't be good!"

Malvaron's hologram face appeared above Arkayna's
phone, looking confused. "Yeah, I know. News reports are
already starting to come in."

"Oh my goblin," Arkayna gasped. "Girls, we have
to hurry!" She turned back to the phone as the griffins
launched into the air. "Where are they attacking?"

"Well, that's the thing," Malvaron said. "They're not, really."

"What?"

"Here, I'll show you." Arkayna's phone blooped as Malvaron sent her a video.

Ten feet away, clinging to Archer's back, Zarya watched as Arkayna's brow furrowed. "Hey, Malvaron, don't leave the rest of us out!" Zarya yelled over.

She heard a muffled "Oh, sorry!" A second later, her own phone blooped, and she gestured to start the video.

In the short clip, shot by a bystander at street level, three spectres swooped down to the side of a tall office building, stopping to hover about six stories up. Ignoring screams from below, they peered in one glass window after another, until one of the spectres pointed and screeched. Together, the three battered the window with their weapons until it broke. Then they reached inside, grabbed something with their bony arms, and flapped away.

"What the hex?" Zarya looked at the other Mysticons, who were watching with similar confused expressions. She saw Em freeze the video on her phone and zoom in on the spectres.

"Cords, maybe?" said Em, puzzled. "It looks like they grabbed a bunch of cords."

Bloop. Another video arrived on their phones. In this one, three other spectres landed in a junkyard and grabbed armloads of scrap metal.

Bloop. Another video. Two spectres pointed long spears at three terrified doctors as a third spectre ransacked an emergency room. Then the three spectres flew away with a bunch of bottles and packets wrapped in a sheet, leaving the doctors unharmed.

Bloop. Three spectres herded terrified comet-watchers into a corner at the Mercer Observatory, then three more descended from the sky, pried open the upturned end of the largest telescope, and carefully pulled out its huge curved lens.

Zarya massaged her temple as the videos kept coming in. There must be a pattern. Metal, cords, lenses . . . Suddenly, she remembered the neat crates of materials in Ami's wagon, and she gasped. "I know what they're doing!"

"For realsies?" Piper said, a hint of awe in her voice. "You *are* so smart!"

"Well, I don't know *exactly* what they're doing," Zarya admitted, "but I bet they're getting stuff for Ami." She grimaced. "The spectres aren't the threat this time. Whatever she's building is."

Arkayna nodded and addressed her phone again. "Malvaron, where are the spectres taking everything?"

"I'm not sure yet," he said, and then he blinked, looking at something in front of him. "But I have a pretty good guess."

Part of Zarya didn't even want to know. She braced herself, and still she was surprised.

"The royal guards are reporting that a huge skeleton bird just landed on the castle balcony," Malvaron continued. "You'd better get back here."

In Which a Plan Becomes a Threat

20

AMILETH PUT BOTH HANDS TO THE SMALL OF HER BACK AND
stretched, then bent over her project again. There wasn't
much time, and there would be only one chance at this.

She was briefly distracted by the noises around her.
From where she worked, crouching several feet back from
the edge of the wide balcony, she could hear the crowd
below. Guards were keeping everyone behind a barrier set
back from the castle, not sure what kind of threat was
inside, but they weren't evacuating the plaza completely.
Ami was pleased; the more people stayed out in the open,
the better her device would work.

She heard a *clunk* behind her and glanced over her shoulder, where an open arch led directly into the castle. Dreadbane and the spectres, their errands finished, had taken a handful of guards hostage and set up a defensive line around the . . . Ami couldn't actually tell what kind of room it was supposed to be. Some kind of lounge, maybe? Did lounges usually have giant, dangling chandeliers and tasseled furniture? In any case, the spectres had pushed the furniture up against the walls, giving Ami more room to work, and the hostages huddled in one corner with Dreadbane looming over them. In the opposite corner, the skeletal vulture lurked, pecking at the shiny tassels on the couches. The sound Ami had heard was one of its huge wings knocking over a table.

Ami shuddered. The bird gave her the creeps. She didn't feel great about Dreadbane threatening the hostages, either. Sternly, she reminded herself that they'd be fine in a couple of hours. She looked up at the approaching comet and smiled grimly. *Everything* would be fine in a couple of hours.

Picking up a screwdriver, she refocused on the device in front of her. On the outside, it looked like a crudely cobbled together version of one of her anti-magic footlights, but about three times as large. And the inside held a few surprises.

Once she plugged in this light, the beam, focused through the giant telescope lens, would be strong enough to reach the comet. Like any other light that hit Wells's Comet, it would split and refract and reflect back down, hitting thousands of points all over the city. But unlike other lights, anything touched by these reflected beams would have the magic sucked out of it. And unlike her stage act, where magic was stored safely in her normal footlights, this targeted magic would be siphoned off into the sky and lost forever.

She finished screwing the giant lens into its metal frame, slotted it into place at the front of the device, and began cleaning it carefully with the alcohol and sterile cloths from the emergency room. Only a couple more steps to go.

And then, she thought, *no more will a few random people be given huge amounts of power, while the rest of us are left to dream of an easier life.* Once Ami had taken their magic, everyone would be on equal footing, to find their own way using their own talents. It would be good for them. *After all, how can you know what you're capable of,* she thought as she lifted the light onto its stand, *until you're forced to try?* If she could do it, so could they.

With the lens clean and the device in place, there was only one piece missing. On the ground in front of her, resting on a clean cloth, was a palm-size, flat, polished piece of glass. With it, she could test the aim and reach of the device. She looked around to make sure no one was paying attention, then patted the inside pocket of her jacket, where she had hidden one of her crystal prisms, the same size as the glass. The prism was the product of hundreds of hours of trial and error. It was the key to her anti-magic beams, allowing light to resonate on a frequency that magic responded to. This small, fragile trinket, and the others like it that were still installed in her stage footlights, were the most closely guarded secret of her life. So she would install the prism at the last moment, only when she was sure everything else was ready. After reassuring herself that the prism was intact, she picked up the test glass and opened the back of the device, revealing an empty slot. Then she froze.

The noises from the crowd below had changed. Before, they had been anxious murmurs. But now, growing slowly in both volume and intensity, she heard . . . cheering?

"Stop right there, Amileth!" the Dragon Mage demanded. In tight formation, four griffins flew down to ring the balcony, and the Mysticons leapt off and landed dramatically on the railing.

Amileth rolled her eyes, allowing magic to begin building in the fingers of her free hand. *Time to teach these girls another lesson,* she thought.

In Which Alliances Shift and Create a New Rift

21

EM HAD LANDED CLOSEST TO THE DEVICE, AND NOW SHE
peered at it from her perch on the railing. "That thing's
pointed right at the comet," she realized.

"The comet is made of magic?" Piper gasped. "Then the
light'll kill it! Don't take Wells's Comet away, Amileth,"
she pleaded. "What'd it ever do to you?"

Ami shook her head, grinning slyly. "Try again, little
one. But hurry, I have very little time for you right now."

"You have more time than you think," Arkayna said.
She pointed to the device. "Mysticon Knight, take it
apart."

"Touch my work and you'll regret it," Ami snarled. She gestured, and a ball of blue energy began to grow and crackle in her hand.

Em froze, looking from Arkayna to Ami.

Zarya jumped into the silence, slinging her bow across her back and climbing down from the rail. She held her hands out in front of her. "Ami, whatever you're thinking of doing, just listen. Dreadbane is dangerous."

"He's the least dangerous person I've met tonight," Ami said. "But that will change soon."

"Not if—" Arkayna began challengingly.

"Dragon Mage!" interrupted Zarya. She stared at Arkayna, willing all her fear and desperation to show in her eyes. "Let me."

Arkayna exhaled and nodded.

Zarya turned back to Ami. "What do you mean, 'that will change soon'?"

"Soon, all of the magic that you sling around so irresponsibly will be gone," Amileth said. "All of the magic in the *city* will be gone." She nodded. "And then everything will be much simpler. Much better."

"*WHAT?*" cried Zarya. "Ami, you're going to hurt a lot of people!"

"I'm—Don't exaggerate. Some people will feel helpless until they learn to live without their magic, yes. But—"

"No, Ami, think it through, please," Zarya said. "You won't just be taking the magic out of *people*."

"Some of the medical equipment in the hospital runs on magic," Em pointed out.

"The Dragon Train runs on magic!" cried Piper. "It'll crash for sure—*boom!*"

"Plus everyone's phones will stop working . . ." Arkayna started.

"Scry-fi will fail . . ." continued Em.

"Exactly," finished Zarya. "And that's just the start. There's gonna be sickness and chaos and panic. How will that make anything better?"

Ami took a step backward. "I . . . You're just trying to stall me. Again!"

Zarya shook her head. "Look, I get it. We treated you badly. You wanted us to know that, and we do. We're so sorry. But what you're planning is . . . well, it's not *you*."

Ami let out a bark of angry laughter. "Oh, and you know me so well," she scoffed.

"I know what you told me," Zarya said, taking a step closer to Ami. She gestured to the crowd below. "You want to show people that there's more to their lives, right? You want to do what you do best: Make them wonder. *Amaze* them. Right?"

Slowly, Ami nodded.

"This isn't going to do any of that. It's just going to scare them."

Ami looked down at the glass in her hand, and her eyes filled with tears. "You're right. By the stars, you're right. I just felt so betrayed. Since I was a child, I believed that if I could ever do real magic, my troubles would be over. And when the opposite turned out to be true, I—well, I acted rashly." She looked up at Zarya. "I told you I wasn't the best at thinking on my feet."

Zarya nodded. "It's not too late," she said. "Let's just—"

"What's going on out here?" Dreadbane demanded, striding onto the balcony, sword in hand.

"Dreadbane," said Ami, spinning to face him, "we can't do this. I didn't realize how many people I would hurt." She held her chin up bravely. "I won't go through with it."

"Oh, it's far too late for that," snickered Dreadbane.

"But this won't do what we wanted! It won't prove to

everyone that magic only causes trouble. In fact, it'll probably do the opposite!"

"You think I'm concerned what people *think*?" Dreadbane shook his head, amused. "Not at all. I only care what they *do*, and I tell you, I have been hurt by magic one too many times." He shook his fist at the sky. "After this, I will finally be free of *her* magic, which has brought me nothing but pain!"

Confused, Ami pointed at the Mysticons, mouthing, *Does he mean one of you?*

The Mysticons all shook their heads in unison, and Arkayna mouthed back, *Necrafa.*

Ami raised her eyebrows as the pieces clicked into place for her. "Ohhhh, he was hurt by *Necrafa*," she breathed.

Dreadbane growled in rage. "Don't you dare speak her name!"

He lunged for Ami, his eyes locked on the glass piece in her hand.

In Which a Chase Gets Chilly

22

BEFORE ANYONE COULD REACT, DREADBANE SNATCHED THE glass roughly away from Ami, then reared back to cut her down with his sword.

WHOOM! A green energy dome slammed into place over Dreadbane, and the blow meant for Ami's head was absorbed by the force field instead.

"Let's go, Amileth!" Arkayna yelled, lowering her arm. "That won't hold him for long!"

Zarya helped a slightly stunned Ami onto Archer's back as Dreadbane smashed at the force field with his sword, screaming for backup.

"You could have left me," Ami told her.

"Not a chance," Zarya said, grinning. "We're heroes, remember?"

With the Mysticons and Ami safely on the griffins' backs, they launched from the balcony just as the undead vulture flapped out onto it. A second later, Arkayna's energy dome shattered with a crash. Dreadbane leapt atop the vulture and took off in pursuit of the Mysticons.

"He's coming!" called Em.

"The device won't work!" Ami called back. "But he doesn't know that!"

Arkayna urged Izzie on. "We need to get Ami away from him!"

"The Undercity?" Zarya suggested.

"I have a *way* more fun idea," Piper giggled, pointing below them.

If Wellsnight had been going to plan, the plaza would have been cleared out by this point, to make room for the dance party. But instead, with the guards pushing everyone back, some of the booths closest to the castle hadn't been completely disassembled yet. Boxes of souvenirs and coolers full of snacks waited next to abandoned trucks. Zarya followed Piper's finger and saw a wide-open truck, mostly full of cartons, with COMET CREAMSICLES written on the side.

At that moment, the vulture chasing them gave out a blood-curdling shriek, and the watching crowd screamed and cowered.

Zarya nodded. "Those folks could use some fun," she said. "I say we go for it. Dragon Mage?"

Arkayna laughed. "Definitely." She patted her griffin. "Go, Izzie!"

The Mysticons' griffins swooped away from the plaza in a long, high arc, and Dreadbane followed on his vulture. Higher and higher they flew, as fast as they could, the vulture straining to keep up with them. Then, in a neat line, they banked around and dove steeply.

Zarya heard Dreadbane's startled "Come back here!" and turned her head to yell, "Catch us if you can, bonehead!"

Infuriated, Dreadbane kicked his mount, who squawked in protest but ducked its head and dropped after them.

Zarya felt Ami's hands tighten on her waist as the plaza got closer and closer. "Hang on tight," she told her. "You don't have to look."

"You think I'd miss this?" Ami replied, the wind of their descent tearing the words out of her mouth. "Not a chance!"

Just when it looked like all four griffins were going to face-plant into the stones of the plaza, they pulled up sharply, pumping their strong wings. Zarya could hear the claws on Archer's feet scrape against the top of the open truck as they barely cleared it before peeling off into the sky again.

Dreadbane's vulture wasn't so flexible. It tried hard to correct its course, but to no avail. It crashed into the back of the truck, and Dreadbane tumbled forward, splatting into a pile of cardboard and half-melted ice cream.

As a cheer went up from the crowd, the Mysticons flew off into the city. When they were sure Dreadbane wasn't following, they had the griffins land on the roof of a skyscraper, and everyone caught their breath.

Ami spoke up after a minute. "He's not done, you know."

Zarya nodded. "I know. So we're going to leave you here while we go back to fight him."

"I—" began Ami, but Zarya cut her off.

"This is my job, not yours. I may not have powers right now, but I'm still a Mysticon."

"But I—" Ami tried again, but now Zarya was turning to Arkayna with a half smile.

"Unless you think I'd slow you down, Dragon Mage?" Zarya asked. Her heartbeat kicked up a notch.

To Zarya's relief, Arkayna shook her head. "Never crossed my mind," she said. "I have no idea how we'd do this without you, powers or no powers."

Ami cleared her throat. "This moment is touching," she said, "but not necessary." Gingerly, she pulled the prism from her pocket. It was beautiful, perfectly faceted, and shimmering with the slightest motion of her hand. "See this?"

Zarya nodded, confused.

"This prism is the key to all my anti-magic lights," Ami continued. "With this, and the device I just built, Zarya . . ." Ami stepped close to Zarya and took her hand, holding the sparkling crystal between them. "I think I can give you back your magic."

In Which Amileth Performs for a Tough Crowd

23

THE GRIFFINS FLEW LOW ALONG SIDE STREETS, HEADED BACK
to the castle. Ami, seated behind Zarya, had explained to
the Mysticons how focused on the device Dreadbane was.
He wouldn't care about coming after them, as long as he
thought he had a chance of completing it himself. So they
all figured that Dreadbane was still at the castle. But it
was only a matter of time before he turned on the device
and found that it didn't work, so they needed to move
quickly.

Their plan depended heavily on Ami, and she was not

happy about that. She shifted on Archer's back, trying to calm down.

Zarya twisted around to look at her. "You're gonna be great," she said. "It's all flash and misdirection, right? You do that all the time!"

"My audience is not usually so angry," Ami replied, "or so heavily armed." She tried to breathe deeply, then shook her head. "I'm too scared. He'll be able to tell."

"Think of it as stage fright," Zarya said. "You get stage fright, right? How do you beat it?"

Ami rolled her eyes a little wildly. "I remind myself how much I've practiced! Practice makes me comfortable! And I haven't practiced this at all!"

"Hey," Zarya said, "I've been meaning to tell you something. You're actually really good at thinking fast. It took you no time to figure out, like, a dozen things to do with my magic once you had it, and you were starting from scratch. Right?"

Ami tipped her head to the side, considering. "That's true."

"See? You're better than you think. And besides, if you freeze, we'll all be there. *I'll* be there." Zarya winked. "I've got your back."

Ami chuckled. "Now *that* makes me feel better." She traced the edges of the prism in her pocket again, then nodded. "All right. I'm ready."

The Mysticons led her into the castle via a back way, and Ami soon lost track of the twists and turns they took through the hallways. The tense royal guards they encountered were quickly soothed by a word from either the Dragon Mage or the Knight. Ami was impressed—the Mysticons *were* respected around here. Soon, they crept toward the bottom of a long, curved stairway. The room that opened onto the balcony was at the top of the stairs, and two fierce-looking spectres stood guard outside the door.

"Okay, now remember," Zarya said to Ami, "if you get in trouble, just yell, and we'll be right there. Otherwise, we'll wait for your cue."

"After we get those two, right?" whispered the Striker, pointing at the spectre guards. "Ooh, they are gonna get *hooped*!"

Ami grinned. She did like the Striker's spirit. "I'll leave you to that, then," she said, brushing off her pants and straightening her jacket. "It's showtime." With a confident stride, she approached the bottom of the stairs.

The spectres recognized her immediately and screeched at her to halt. Obediently, Ami raised her hands. "Tell Dreadbane I have returned," she commanded.

One of the spectres stuck its head inside the room and shrieked; a few seconds later it motioned her inside. As Ami stepped through the doorway, she heard a *clink* from the bottom of the stairs. The two spectres on guard startled and began creeping cautiously toward the noise. *Here comes the hooping*, Ami thought, biting her lip to hide her smile.

Pulling the door closed behind her, she found herself inches from the tip of Dreadbane's cruel-looking sword as he pointed it at her face. "Well," he sneered, "this is unexpected."

Ami forced herself to laugh. "Really? You know the Mysticons, surely. After five minutes in their company, I knew I'd made a mistake." Through the closed door at her back, she heard a clatter, and she cleared her throat to cover it. "That device," she continued, pointing out to the balcony, "is my greatest achievement. It would be folly to leave it behind without seeing what it can do. And without me, you'll never make it work."

Dreadbane tipped his head to the side skeptically. "How did you get past the castle guards?"

Ami focused the tension in her body into her eyes, and from Dreadbane's reaction she knew they had begun to glow and spark blue. "I am very persuasive these days," she replied.

Chuckling, Dreadbane lowered his sword. "As long as you're here, you might as well stay." He made a motion, and two more spectres closed in behind Ami, blocking the door. "Don't test my patience further."

She glanced around. The other two dozen spectres ringed the room, standing watchful but at ease. The skeletal vulture, still dripping with ice cream in spots, was back in its favorite corner by the couch. *Calm. Stay calm, and put on the show,* she told herself. She crossed the room and stepped out onto the balcony.

"Now," she said, turning back to Dreadbane, "this device may look complete, but it is not. A few important adjustments have yet to be made."

Dreadbane glanced pointedly at the sky, where the comet was now half as large as the moon and sparkling fiercely.

"Happily, it will take just minutes," she finished. "If you'll allow me?"

Dreadbane nodded. "*I* will be the one to turn it on, though," he said. He moved to stand over the device's plug, which was coiled at the end of a five-foot cord.

"Agreed," Amileth said with a wave. She opened the back of the device. "First let's make sure that you installed the last piece correctly."

"Do you take me for a fool? Of course I did!" Dreadbane snarled.

"Of course you did," agreed Ami soothingly. "Still, it can't hurt to check." Turning her body to block Dreadbane's view, she quickly popped the glass piece out of the slot, palmed it, and inserted the prism in its place. "Well done," she told him, closing up the device again and moving to the front. "And now for the adjustments. I'll of course have to make them from the inside."

She unscrewed and lifted off the giant lens in its frame, setting it aside. Then she reached forward with her left hand, as if fiddling with one of the cords inside the barrel. Keeping her eyes locked on the device and muttering nonsense instructions to herself to keep Dreadbane distracted, she concentrated and crooked her right hand. Feeling the invisible energy uncoiling from her fingers, she aimed—oh, this was much harder when she wasn't looking directly at her target—and lashed out with her mind. *There.* She had definitely caught something with her magic whip.

"Done!" she called, holding up her empty left hand with a flourish. She saw Dreadbane's eyes follow her motion, chose her moment, and . . . *now.* She clenched her right hand and yanked.

Inside the room, the chain holding up the chandelier suddenly shattered, and the huge crystal structure crashed to the ground. Dreadbane spun to look, and all the spectres in the room jumped. In the next instant, the doors were thrown open, and the Mysticons charged in.

Dreadbane roared in anger and turned toward Ami, but the Dragon Mage demanded his full attention, lobbing green energy blasts one after another at his head. While he parried and dodged, the Striker and the Knight took on the spectres. The Striker bobbed and weaved, throwing her hoops at one and jumping up to kick the head of another, which made it stumble directly into the path of a third. The Knight, energy shield up, methodically carved her way through another knot of spectres with her flame-shaped sword. And Zarya . . .

Ami watched with admiration as Zarya darted in last, nimbly finding her way over and through the knots of fighters, swiftly moving around the perimeter of the room toward her.

Which reminded Ami—she had another job. Tipping the long barrel of her device down so she was looking directly into it, Ami concentrated again and reached out with the blue energy coil. This time she let the whip be visible as it snaked out and wrapped around the device's power cord.

She looked up, locking eyes with Zarya. "Now?" she asked.

"Now!" Zarya yelled.

Ami chopped her hand down, and the plug sank directly into the outlet in the balcony floor. *Whrrrrrrmm MMMMMMM.* The device powered up, and its light caught her full in the chest. Immediately, the whip dissolved, and Ami felt a strange tugging sensation. *There it goes*, she thought with a mixture of sadness and relief.

She looked up to see Zarya on the balcony. Dreadbane

took a swipe at her as she came close, but Zarya ducked inside his attack, grabbed his shoulder, and used his momentum to spin herself, vaulting away from him and landing next to Ami.

Ami wanted to applaud, but instead she dropped and rolled, leaving Zarya alone in the light. Ami kicked out with her foot and knocked the power cord away from its socket.

Vvvvrrrrrmmmmm. The device wound itself down again, and as it did Zarya's whole body hummed. She tipped her head back and grinned with delight as a wave of blue magic swept over her from head to toe. Her face paint and homemade costume were replaced with a sleek blue-and-white outfit, and a glowing bow appeared in her hand. She opened her eyes and locked her gaze on Amileth.

Ami smiled and dipped her head in greeting. "Mysticon Ranger, I presume?"

In Which One Team Comes Together and
Another Falls Apart

24

DREADBANE LOOKED FROM AMI TO ZARYA, CONFUSED. "WHAT just happened?" Then he focused on the device. "Never mind. My revenge is ready!"

Standing, Ami cleared her throat and smirked. "Not anymore," she said, holding up her hand. In it, she held the glass piece.

"How did you—Give it to me!" Dreadbane snarled. He stepped menacingly toward her.

"Catch!" Ami yelled as she flipped the piece to Zarya, who caught it easily.

Zarya held up the glass and waggled it tauntingly. She stepped backward, jumped up on the balcony railing, and stepped off into the air . . . landing right on Archer's back where he waited below. In seconds, the other Mysticons had disengaged from the spectres and leapt onto their own waiting griffins.

"Not again!" Dreadbane howled, climbing onto his slightly sticky vulture. "This time," he told it, "catch them!"

The vulture squawked and took off.

"Follow and attack!" Dreadbane ordered the spectres as he flew in pursuit. "Get that piece!"

Soon, Ami was alone on the balcony. She watched as the battle began in the air overhead. She had no magic, and no way to help. *Now what?* she thought.

Zarya, flying along on Archer, laughed as the spectres descended toward her. She nocked arrow after arrow, shooting them out perfectly on target. She even managed to pin one spectre's wing to that of its neighbor, sending them both plummeting as they frantically tried to untangle themselves. "I'm back!" she crowed.

"You're back, you're back, you're back!" Piper sang next to her. "Best night ever!"

"Focus, girls," said Arkayna, but she was laughing, too. "We haven't won yet."

Zarya looked over her shoulder to see Dreadbane bearing down on them. He gestured, and a hail of bone shards flew out of his hand. "Look out!" she cried.

The griffins dropped as one, and the shards flew over their heads. They banked around and doubled back, heading underneath Dreadbane's vulture and back over the palace.

Em pulled an orb from her pouch and tossed it overhand. It caught on the vulture's foot and exploded, sending bits of bone raining down on the balcony where Ami still stood. When the smoke cleared, the vulture was missing a foot, but it didn't seem bothered in the slightest.

Em sighed. "I thought that would be more dramatic," she admitted.

Ami covered her head as bone showered down around her. She reached up to ruffle her pouf, and bone dust sifted out of her hair. She tightened her lips in disgust.

Then she froze, one hand still in her hair. She looked from the device to her powdery hand, and then up to where the comet glittered in the sky.

She had an idea.

"Uh, what's she doing?" asked Em as the Mysticons dodged another wave of Dreadbane's bone shards.

Zarya followed her gaze. Ami had gathered several pieces of bone into a pile, and now it looked as if she was . . . stomping on them?

"She must *really* hate that bird," Piper decided. "Oop, heads up!" She flung her hoops at a spectre dropping down on them with a long spear, and with a shriek, the skeleton was battered to the side.

"Wait, now she's doing something with the device," said Arkayna, a hint of alarm in her voice.

Zarya looked again. Sure enough, Ami had opened the back of the device and was reaching inside.

"On the left!" Em shouted, and the griffins banked right to avoid another hail of shards.

"We can't worry about Ami," Zarya called. "We have to focus, or we're going to lose this fight."

Arkayna hesitated, then nodded. "You're right." She locked eyes with Zarya. "I trust you." Together, the Mysticons charged back into the battle.

Please let this work, please let this work, please let this work, Ami thought desperately. She had never tried anything like this before, and the stakes were so high. If only there were time for a test run, but no. Carefully, she spread the vulture's powdered bone over the crystal prism. *The bone is infused with Dreadbane's magic. If I get the coating right, the light will pull out only the magic that Dreadbane has cast. But the prism has to be completely coated, or . . .* She shook her head. She didn't want to think about what would happen if she missed a spot.

She checked the sky again. It was time. The comet was at its closest. On a normal Wellsnight, the dance party would be starting right about now. Instead, the anxious partygoers huddled behind barricades in the plaza below, and the lights flashing in the sky were the Mysticons, valiantly fighting enemies that outnumbered them six to one.

I can help with that. Ami moved to the front of the

device, reattaching the giant lens and tightening it into place. She swiveled the barrel to point directly at the comet. As she reached for the plug, she saw that her hands were shaking. *That won't do*, she thought, and commanded her hands to still. Then, with a grin and a flourish befitting the Amazing Amileth, she plugged in the light.

FWOOOOOOM. The beam shot into the sky, startling Mysticons, Dreadbane, and spectres alike. Zarya's heart skipped a beat as the light hit the comet, split into a million smaller fragments, and came bouncing down to touch all around them.

"*Ah-HA*," Dreadbane hissed in triumph. "She didn't need that last piece after all. She fooled you—ah!" A bone came falling from the sky and clonked him on the head. He looked up and grimaced as, one after another, his spectres started to fall apart around him. "Yes, of course. My army is but a small price to pay for . . ." He trailed off as he saw the Mysticons, pinpoints of light dancing across them, charging at him in formation.

"No! How do you still have your powers? HOW?" he screamed. Then the light hit his vulture, and with one last squawk it began to crumble beneath him. Desperately, Dreadbane stood on its back, and, with a mighty leap, he launched himself at the Mysticons.

But Zarya was ready. She fired two arrows at the approaching Dreadbane, and they exploded off his breastplate and sent him spinning in midair.

With a cry of dismay, Dreadbane plummeted toward the city. A Dragon Train passed below him as he fell, and he hit the roof of the train with a *crunch*. Before the Mysticons could fully grasp what had happened, Dreadbane's unconscious body was carried away, deep into the city.

In Which a Long Night Ends Well,
and a New Day Begins Even Better

25

WITH A ROAR OF APPROVAL, THE CROWD BELOW BURST
through the barriers and swarmed the plaza. The light
show continued as the comet refracted the light from
Ami's device into twinkling beams in every color of the
rainbow that danced over Drake City. The DJs quickly got
the music going, but soon it was drowned out by
chanting.

"Mys-ti-cons! Mys-ti-cons!" the crowd shouted, clapping in time, their heads tipped back to cheer for the
heroes flying above.

Zarya looked toward the castle. Standing at the

balcony railing, laughing as she clapped and chanted along, was Amileth.

Zarya turned to the other girls. "You all head down," she said. "I'll be there in a minute."

Piper pointed a finger at her. "You better be," she said, "because the only thing better than a Wellsnight dance party is a Wellsnight dance party *for us*!"

"I promise," Zarya replied.

"Hey, sis?" said Arkayna. "Tell her thanks. I'm not sure how she did that, but it was . . . well, it was pretty amazing."

"I will." Zarya nodded and steered Archer toward the balcony. She hopped off the griffin's broad back and landed easily next to Ami.

There was a moment of silence, and then they both said, "So . . ."

After another beat, they dissolved into laughter. Pulling herself together, Ami said, "Well, Princess, it's been quite a night."

"I don't know how you're ever going to top this show," Zarya replied.

"Oh, I've already got some fantastic ideas," said Ami.

"When I come back on my next tour, you can tell me what you think of them."

"You've got a deal. But you don't have to go yet, right?" Zarya gestured down to the party, which was kicking into high gear. "This is for you, too."

"I'll stay for a bit," Ami said. "But then I'll slip out. You know what they say in show business: Always leave them wanting more."

"Well then, no time to waste," Zarya said. "Let's dance!"

A little while later, Zarya found Arkayna in the crowd. Together they stood to the side, watching Piper and Em happily crowd surf while a Gnomez 2 Men anthem blared over the speakers.

After a moment, Zarya said, "You know, we never finished our talk from before."

Arkayna tensed. "I know."

Zarya hesitated, then put an arm around Arkayna's shoulders. "I'm really sorry."

Arkayna started. "*You're* sorry? I'm the one who made you feel like I didn't trust you!"

"And I acted like a real jerk trying to prove that I didn't need you." Zarya sighed, then said, "But you know I do."

Arkayna put her arm around Zarya's waist. "I'm sorry I worry too much."

"I'm sorry I get so defensive."

Arkayna smiled, but it was a little sad. "I guess we really do think differently, huh?"

"But that's the thing." Zarya squeezed Arkayna's shoulder. "We don't have everything in common. But we . . . you know."

"We love each other."

"Yeah. And we *get* each other."

Arkayna laughed. "Most of the time."

"Right. And I think that's more important. Don't you?"

The sadness disappeared, and now Arkayna's smile was open and light. "I do," she said, and she hugged Zarya tight, just as dawn broke over the horizon.

Arms around each other, the sisters watched the sun come up. *This really has been a great night*, thought Zarya. She had her magic and her city and her friends, and she had her sister by her side. And standing there with Arkayna, she was sure: Anything that looked like it could drive them apart?

Well, that was all just smoke and mirrors.

ABOUT THE AUTHOR

Liz Marsham began her storytelling career as an editor for DC Comics and Disney Publishing. She lives in Los Angeles with her husband, a cat who thinks she is a princess, and a cat who thinks he is a dog. Visit her (and the cats) at lizmarsham.com.

DISCOVER OTHER
MYSTICONS ADVENTURES!